# LILITH ENRAPTURED

DIVINITY WARRIORS

MICHELLE M. PILLOW

MICHELLE M. PILLOW® - MICHELLEPILLOW.COM

Lilith Enraptured © Copyright 2009 - 2017, Michelle M. Pillow

Fourth Print Edition July 2018

Third Print Edition September 2017

Second Print Edition July 2012

First Print Edition July 2009

Second Electronic Printing January 2012

First Electronic Printing March 2009

ISBN-13: 978-1-62501-191-6

Published by The Raven Books LLC

# ABOUT LILITH ENRAPTURED

## DIVINITY WARRIORS BOOK ONE

*Alternate Reality Romance*

Sorin of Firewall lives in a land forever at war. In fact, the Starian men are so busy fighting, their marriage ceremony has been reduced to a "will of the gods" event where they simply pick a woman out of a lineup and claim her as a wife. With women becoming scarce, it's necessary to trade the offworld Divinity Corporation for brides. Duty-bound to attend the ceremony, he has no intention of picking a bride, let alone one from another dimension. That is, until he sees Lilith, the bewitching woman sent by the gods to reward—or punish?—him.

# ABOUT DIVINITY WARRIORS SERIES

In a land forever at war, the Starian men are so busy fighting that their marriage ceremony has been reduced to a "will of the gods" event where they simply pick a woman out of a lineup and claim her as a wife. With women becoming scarce, it's necessary to trade the offworld Divinity Corporation for brides.

They live a very Medieval-like existence. Instead of medical advancement and technology, all of their focus has been on developing weaponry and battle strategy. With places named for war, such as Spearhead and Battlewar, these men have been left in charge way too long. They are in desperate need of a woman's touch.

DIVINITY SERIES

## Divinity Warriors

## Divinity Healers

The Playful Prince
The Bound Prince
The Rogue Prince
The Pirate Prince

## Captured by a Dragon-Shifter Series

Determined Prince
Rebellious Prince
Stranded with the Cajun
Hunted by the Dragon
Mischievous Prince
Headstrong Prince

## Space Lords Series

His Frost Maiden
His Fire Maiden
His Metal Maiden
His Earth Maiden
His Woodland Maiden

**Qurilixen Lords Series**

Dragon Prince

Marked Prince

*More Coming Soon!*

To learn more about the Qurilixen World series of books and to stay up to date on the latest book list visit www.MichellePillow.com

# AUTHOR UPDATES

To stay informed about when a new book in the series installments is released, sign up for updates:

michellepillow.com/author-updates

"THE FASTER YOU make them come, the less time you must spend in their presence," Sera whispered, her words accented with an unfamiliar intonation. The tight fit of her white corset top squeezed her healthy waist and thrust up two very generous breasts. Long blue skirts billowed around her legs. She eyed the half dozen girls in the cell as she handed them loaves of bread. The need to be helpful shone from her sincere expression. "That is all they want—a vessel to find release in. Do not expect tenderness, but if you don't deny them, if you don't resist, you'll be treated fairly enough. And if you give them sons, you'll be greatly rewarded. Life here is not so bad."

Lilith Grian didn't move. She was still trying to

get over the fact that she'd gone to bed in her own, lonely San LoFrancis apartment and awoke to find herself kidnapped and locked away in some small cell packed full of terrified women, with nothing but a long white robe over her body. The thick wool and shapeless design was a little to "sacrificial" for her tastes. A sniffle sounded next to her and Lilith glanced at the dark-haired woman crying next to her.

"This isn't happening, this isn't happening," the woman repeated, over and over. "Wake up, Edith, wake up."

Almost pleading, Sera shoved a loaf of bread toward Lilith. "I'm telling you how to best survive this place, please, listen. Spreading your thighs is an easy enough task for a decent life. Don't bring trouble upon yourself. Let them find release. They are not such boars when they get what they want."

Edith continued to rock herself, refusing bread and becoming more hysterical with every breath. Lilith wasn't sure who "they" were, but she sure as hell didn't like them already. Unlike Edith, she wasn't upset about the whole inter-dimensional travel scenario. As an historical and cultural analyst for the Divinity Corporation, it was her duty to jump from one plane of existence to another and collect intelligence on that world. She loved discovering the different intricate paths of the human experience, how one tiny event could change the course of humanity. What did concern Lilith was the fact that this jump wasn't assigned, and she was supposed to have two weeks off pending a board review of her last screwed-up mission.

Since Divinity had the only known source of top secret inter-dimensional travel technology on her plane, she guessed that maybe the review wasn't going her way. That or someone wanted her gone. Out of the four-hundred-thirty-six known dimensions, she didn't recognize this one as being charted, but to be fair it was difficult to determine much from inside a prison cell. As an analyst, Lilith had traveled to and studied most of the parallel planes. From what Sera described and the way everyone was dressed, this was new territory.

*They shipped me off to an uncharted dimension?*

Shock at her surroundings turned to outrage. This wasn't an accident. She would have had to have been drugged to be dressed in this outfit and sent through the portal unaware. Natural slips were extremely rare and completely predictable by the company. Sure as sunshine, a portal would not have opened up in her bedroom.

*How dare they! One fuck-up that wasn't even my fault and I'm suddenly exiled?*

She wondered how human this reality was. Some had vampires and werewolves, some had faeries and gnomes, and some had humanoids so alien her dimension's species were hardly compatible. Many of them had never even heard of dimensional travel or portals. Some societies were obsessed to the point of compulsion, some with power, some with medical advancement and some with gladiator fights to the death.

"I can't be here," Edith whispered, shaking her head as if to make it all go away.

Partly taking pity on the frightened woman and partly desperate to get her to shut up, Lilith asked, "Where are you from?"

"San Francisco," Edith said. "What's going on here? Who are these people? Is this a reality show?"

Lilith ran through possibilities in her mind, trying to narrow down the geography to the right plane. "Is that the United States or Dominative Republic?"

"United States," Edith mumbled, sniffing loudly.

Lilith nodded. No wonder the woman was scared. Her dimension had only theorized alternative realities. They weren't even close to learning how to control them. This would be like time travel to her.

"First, you're not crazy. This is another plane of existence you've stepped into." When the woman only looked confused, Lilith explained, "Looking at a foreign dimension is like looking at your world if it had evolved in a different way. To a point there are many similarities. Languages, generally, are relatively similar. Some people will look the same, but not be the same people. Certain events like natural disasters will be shared. Weather is the same and this is still Earth. These people are still human-ish."

Lilith frowned, studying the iron bars keeping them locked in. Apparently, this particular dimension hadn't made it too far past the Middle Ages—if the trencher to hold the bread, serving wench and barbaric mentality of "just make him come and keep him happy" was any indication.

"You're as crazy as they are," Edith declared, backing away from her.

*So much for helping out my fellow humanoid.*

The other women in the cell held themselves quiet. Each wore the white, shapeless dress with bare feet. A blonde woman whimpered pathetically, watching as a tall, black-haired woman paced in front of her as if she might pounce. The dark-skinned beauty strode with amazing grace and poise, much like a dancer or martial artist.

A redhead merely sat, staring at the bars as if she knew exactly what was happening and where she was. Her fingers picked absentmindedly at the long sleeve of her gown. She hadn't moved since they woke up that morning. The last prisoner, a well-endowed brunette, had pulled a thin metal clip out of her upswept hair and thrust it into the outside lock, trying to work the door free.

Suddenly, the brunette jerked her hand back and thrust the clip into her hair. A burly man dressed in a hard leather jerkin and dark breeches approached the cells, standing between the bars and the blue-grey stone wall on the other side of the narrow hall. Metal diamonds plated the leather, creating a symmetrical pattern over his thick chest. The guard crossed his thick arms, creating a veritable blockade more effective than the iron.

Lilith knew how to defend herself if the need arose, but he would be a hard opponent to beat. Well, to be honest, she hadn't actually practiced her defensive moves like she should have been according to Divinity employee policy. Her punches would only do so much damage and he had the muscle mass to absorb her blows with ease. A long, thin scar traced down the side of his cheek, adding a dangerous appeal to his look. Edith and the blonde whimpered. Lilith couldn't help but note that maybe she was the only one who thought the man appealing.

The warrior guard studied them one by one, not appearing pleased with what he saw. Then, motioning to the side, he beckoned another warrior man to appear next to him. "The flaxen one and the crying one. They do not carry themselves well. Take them and give them the philter."

Lilith automatically touched a lock of her straight, blonde hair. Her heart jumped a little in her chest, until she saw the guard look at the other flaxen-headed woman.

"What?" Edith screamed. "No, wait! I'll be good. I swear I'll be good. Please, don't hurt me. Please, I'll do anything you want. Do you want me to make you come? I will. I swear I will. I'll do you all!" To disprove her point, her body began to shake and she started bawling anew.

The guard looked disgusted by her display. Lilith couldn't say she blamed him. Where was the woman's honor? Her pride? If death was to come, there was nothing to be gained by tears. What she should be doing is analyzing their environment and calculating her escape.

The barred door opened and four men filed inside. Their massive warrior-like presence made her feel tiny in comparison as they crowded the cell. Two grabbed the now sobbing Edith and dragged her out. The blonde screamed, kicking and fighting as tears streamed down her face. The four remaining women held perfectly still. Lilith did not want to be grabbed next. The gods only knew what this "philter" was. It didn't sound pleasant.

As soon as the men were gone, the brunette went back to work, her face set as she tried to feel around the lock with her hairpin. The cell became eerily quiet now that the two women had been taken away.

"You won't be able to open it," the redhead said, staring at the lock picker. "Even if you did, there would be no escape. You'd have to fight through the warriors' hall, out of the guarded castle gates and run three strikes over open prairie until you reach the forest. Should you survive the wild beasts that live there, you'd soon find yourself prisoner to an even more vicious race of creatures—monsters so fierce and depraved they'll make you beg for death. Trust me, with the war going on in this forsaken place, we're in the better of the two sides."

"Who are you that we should trust what you say?" the brunette asked.

"Name's Paige," the redhead answered.

"Lilith," Lilith inserted, glad they'd finally started communicating. She didn't blame them for being cautious. All morning there had been a secret judging and assessing between them.

"What do they want with us?" The black-haired woman stopped pacing. All eyes turned to her. "Oh, I'm called Jayne."

"They want us to be their whores," Paige answered, bitterness seeping into her hard tone. "They don't call it that, but that's what they want—a subservient woman to rub their feet and spread her legs. If you don't, they get pissed and the whole lot of them stares at you like you are demon spawn incarnate and blames you for your chosen warrior's bad mood. It's either fuck them and suck them, or you're treated like the bottom rung of Starian society."

"Again, I ask, why should we trust you? We don't know you." The brunette continued to try to pick the lock. "You could be a plant sent here to make us behave with horror stories of what's beyond the tree line."

"I don't care if you trust me, but I know what I'm talking about. This isn't my first time in a cage." Paige tilted her head back and sighed. "They'll be coming to get us soon."

"What's your name, locksmith?" Jayne asked the brunette.

"Karre."

"Well, Karre," Jayne said, "I don't think we have much of a choice. If we all work together, maybe we stand a chance. Now, I don't know how we all got here and at this point I don't think it matters, but I do know I'm not staying to spend the rest of my life as some guy's sex toy."

"I agree." Lilith stood, hoping Jayne would have a logical solution they could use. "We need a plan."

"Fine," Karre grumbled.

Paige opened her eyes and shook her head. "Don't look to me to join your little band. You're only fooling yourselves. I've been to the Hanging Forest. I made it all the way to the Starian borders and I've seen the creatures that wait beyond."

"What about a dimension jump?" Lilith asked. "Does anyone know if this place has inter-dimensional travel technology?"

"A what?" Paige furrowed her brow in confusion.

"Staria? It's too primitive. They don't have the technology here," Karre said. "I got a glimpse of the castle when they brought me to this cell. Through a door I saw servants cart water from a well in buckets and the drive wasn't paved. No artificial lights or motorized vehicles. Though there were several large horses."

"I've never been here," Jayne contributed, "but I'm inclined to agree from what I've observed. These prisons don't use lasers or shocks."

"Someone's coming." Karre pulled her arms out from between the bars. She thrust her lock-picking tool back into her upswept hair.

A new guard arrived, dressed similar to the other men she'd seen. His nose had a crook across the bridge. He frowned. "Only three new ones?"

"It's all they sent us," said the man who'd ordered the other two women away.

"How's it going, Edward?" Paige taunted, her face hardening to hide all emotion. "I see the nose is healing nicely."

"Lady Paige," Edward growled, glaring at her as if he wanted to pull the sword from his waist and run her through.

"Open the door, Eddie," Paige taunted. "Let me break it again."

Edward grumbled, but didn't answer.

"I thought there were five new," another of Edward's fellow barbarians said, completely ignoring Paige.

"What's wrong, Brock? Don't I count anymore in

your little ledger?" Paige taunted. Lilith kept quiet, observing as was her nature to do.

"You are not new," Brock stated, frowning at her in disapproval. "Your lord is waiting for you and I do hope his punishment is harsh."

Paige's smirk faltered. Brock grinned victoriously.

"You already have one of these guys?" Karre whispered, grabbing Paige's arm.

"Two were not suitable. They were taken away," Edward said, answering his companion. His nostrils flared in distaste. "Too weak."

"Three will have to do," Brock answered, sighing. As the two men walked off, he added, "I'll tell my Sera to make ready."

A long silence filled the cell, broken only when Paige whispered, "Ladies, welcome to Battlewar Castle."

IF LORD SORIN HATED ANYTHING, he hated waste —wasted resources, wasted hours, wasted lives. And, as far as he was concerned, these breeding cere-monies were a waste of time. Nothing in the process of prancing women before the warriors, who then picked them based on an urge, guaranteed a well-made match. Their ancestors had the right idea when they'd raided villages and took the women they wanted. At least the raids served three purposes—the need for men to find a woman to put into their bed, the need for men to have sons and the need for men to fight their wars. Besides, going on a raid would not take the warriors away from the battlefront, not like traveling back to Battlewar Castle in the northern-most part of their kingdom for a breeding ceremony.

Women were scarce in this hard land. Sons became a necessity and their natural evolution seemed to answer the call with more sons than daughters—when they did have children. Their low birthrate wasn't from lack of trying when the warriors were home, but war took them away all too often. Sometimes forever.

Sorin glanced around his castle chambers, the place he always stayed when he came to Battlewar. Ever since his own castle, Firewall, burned to the ground, this was as close to a stationary home as he had. Like all male rooms, the decorations were sparse —a large bed with a mammoth-wolf fur coverlet, a large wall filled with every weapon he'd ever owned in chronological order, a fireplace, comfortable chair, a trunk for his personal belongings and two doors.

The black stone walls pressed in on him. He shouldn't be here. He should be at the encampment with the other men. What did he care if tradition dictated he at least attempt to take a breeding partner, a mate, a bride, a whatever the women liked to call the joining nowadays. He had a bride once and it did him little good. Bianka, the accursed wench, was dead and it suited him just fine not to replace her.

Still moist from his recent bath, he adjusted his hips on the chair and wrapped his callused fingers around the semi-erect member between his thighs. Granted, self-satisfaction wasn't as gratifying as the real thing, but it would keep his head level during the ceremony. He would never forgive himself if he did something stupid. The longer his kind went without the exhausting pleasure of the bed, the more their moods were said to be altered. Sorin grunted. He thought he did just fine without a woman.

He gripped his cock hard, squeezing in irritation as he tried not to think of how he wanted to be far away from there. It didn't take long for his erection to reach full capacity and begin to ache. Veins strained along the firm flesh, leading a familiar trail over his shaft from thick base to smooth tip. The water dried and the rough texture of his war-hardened hand caused an insistent friction along his shaft. Nothing about the grip reminded him of the soft folds of a woman and that's the way he liked it—hard and empty.

He stroked fast and tight. The muscles in his stomach tightened. His body knew its part and didn't need to be romanced into climaxing. Closing his eyes, he let the end come. Physical release sated one hunger, the feast being prepared below stairs would take care of the other. By morn, he'd ride out with his brother to join the battlefront.

Sorin stood and stretched his hands over his head. The low fire had dried the water from his naked flesh. All this sitting around and reflecting didn't sit well on his mind. Completely comfortable in his nakedness, he strode to the trunk and flung it open. Tradition demanded he dress nicely this evening, even though he much preferred armor to silken threads.

But hate all this nonsense as he may, it was his turn to sit before the stage and watch the newest batch of women being paraded before them. And, like the several times before, he'd do nothing but sit and wait and curse the hours of his life that were being wasted.

## 2

"I say we make a fight of it," Jayne put forth, twisting her arms in an effort to be free of the ropes around her wrists. She'd already put up a good fight as the men came to restrain them in the prison cell. Karre had been no less defiant, though her moves seemed more calculated and her eyes ever watchful. Paige simply held out her hands and let them bind her, as if whatever fight she'd once had disappeared completely.

Lilith clearly wasn't the fighter Jayne was, nor was she the beaten pushover Paige had obviously become. If anything, she was like Karre, watching and waiting, analyzing as she always did on assignment. Only this time there were no safety protocols if she got into trouble. The fact terrified her. She knew self-defense and had been trained in basic survival, but in truth, she was just an analyst. She spent most of her field hours in libraries and tech labs, learning about the different dimensions' individual histories and political systems. Occasionally she'd attend banquets and celebrations, always observing, rarely participating. She collected intelligence, sometimes known by that particular plane's authorities, sometimes not. Her job was to observe and under no circumstances was she to interfere.

So what did all those years of training mean now? Did she fight? Every instinct told her to stay calm and observe, to wait and learn. But was fear making her cling to the familiar? She had to remind herself that this wasn't a mission. This was her life, potentially the rest of her life if she didn't find a way out. There was no safety button hidden in a necklace that would alert the company to come and get her. She was on her own.

No, that wasn't true. She had four potential allies standing right next to her in the same sacrificial white gowns and rope chain accessories.

"Paige already tried fighting and running," Lilith whispered, automatically testing the tight ropes around her wrists. They bit into her flesh, seeming to get tighter the more she pulled at them. A guard stood at the end of a long hall, which passed rows of cells much like the one they'd been kept in. The women made no move to follow the man out of the prison area. "The way I see it, we don't have any choice but to join forces and pool our knowledge. I think we should gather intelligence. None of us seem to be from this world, so that means they had to get us all here somehow. If we keep our ears open, we'll find out how. There might be a way out of here yet."

"I've already looked for fairy rings when I was in the forest," Paige said. "I didn't even find evidence of fairies. Though, I'm not surprised. Fairies don't like wars and this place is nothing but one giant battle-field. I think my journey here was a one-way trip."

"Fairy rings?" Karre snorted with soft laughter.

"What?" Paige asked, looking around at the others. "Isn't that how you all got here?"

"No more talking. They're ready for you," the guard announced, motioning his fist forward. "Let's go. March."

Lilith didn't readily move. The prisons felt oddly safe. Once she stepped out into this world who knew what she'd encounter.

"March!" the guard yelled in irritation.

Lilith jolted, shivering.

"Let me help." Paige tugged on her arm, dragging Lilith forward a few steps before letting go. "Brock's ill-tempered and in the end you'll still be marching out there. Just be glad he's letting you keep the clothes. This is one group you don't want to greet naked."

The women filed out of the prison corridor into a blue-grey stone passageway. This time one of the guards did walk behind them as they followed Brock. Wooden doors with thick metal handles spread out on either side, lit by torches placed on the walls. Material whispered with each step and the sound of their bare feet padding across the cold floor created a steady beat to the harder clomping of the guards' boots. Otherwise, the castle was silent.

The long passageway turned into another, then into another, becoming an endless maze of twists and turns. As the sound of voices penetrated their march, Lilith stared past Karre's shoulder. A new light shone from ahead, brighter than the torches but still flickering like firelight. The nearer they walked toward the light, the louder the sounds became. Rowdy, gruff and very male, the voices caused Lilith to falter in her steps. Paige bumped into her back, only to forcefully push her forward.

Her breathing deepened and her heart raced. Each heavy thump brought her closer to passing out. The firelight began to dance in her vision.

*No!*

Lilith jerked her senses back from the threat of oblivion and steeled her nerves. She might be just an analyst, but she had been trained for tactical situations. She needed to focus. This was a mission. She wasn't being paid for it, but it was perhaps the most important mission she had ever been on.

Holding her head up high, she walked under the narrow archway into a crowded hall. First, she needed to survey her surroundings. Battlewar Castle appeared to be a beefy evolution of the medieval period, honed to perfection by centuries of care, and decorated by men. Lilith had seen castles before and, though they had distinctly different styles, the layouts were generally the same. If it stayed true to common form, there would be a town beyond the inner gate, spread out over the distance and leading to an outer gate.

Warriors watched the four women with interest from the long rows of tables in the main hall. Though gruff in appearance, most of them looked recently bathed. Some wore lightweight tunics, others leather jerkins like the guards, others light chainmail and pieces of armor, and still others wore no shirt at all. Big metal goblets had been set before them, next to matching pitchers. She'd thought the guards were scary, but some of these men were practically gigantic. Muscles bulged, littered with puckered scars and tattooed designs. Despite her best efforts, her heart hammered wildly and her throat became dry. She was expected to sexually satisfy one of these warrior knights? If their cocks were anything like the rest of them, they'd tear her apart.

The light came from a large fireplace along a far side of the room. Like most things in this place, it was immense and towering. Woven tapestries lined the walls in strips of material, showcasing coats-of-arms and various symbols she didn't yet recognize.

"Come on," the guard muttered, his voice not booming like before as he led them through a path made between the tables.

Lilith noticed women mixed in with some of the men. Though not so tight as Sera, they had corset tops clearly designed to entice and enflame their male leaders, and skirts for easy access. A bearded knight licked his lips as she passed, his eyes raking over her as if she were already naked and strapped to the table. She swallowed hard, realizing he wasn't the only one looking at her like that. Lilith wondered if the firelight revealed more of her naked body beneath the white gown than she would have liked. She pulled her arms close.

Sera's words echoed in her head, "The faster you make them come, the less time you must spend in their presence. That is all they want—a vessel to find release in."

Did they expect the women to please all these men? The hungry glances and deepened breathing didn't deny the idea. Tension filled the air and the talking had quieted by small degrees. The prisoners turned and were led forward to the front of the hall. A raised table, set high upon a platform of honor, awaited empty.

"Stand here," Brock ordered, pointing before the tables. Then yelling, he announced, "Bring in the firsts so they may make their choice."

Firsts? Did that mean her worst fear was correct? They would have to pleasure more than one of these giant, warrior men? However would she survive it?

The hall erupted into a crescendo of good-natured laughter and cheering. Six men walked into the main hall, fierce and proud. Their clothes gleamed in a way not seen in the others' clothing. A small detail, to be sure, but it did set these men apart from the others. Each wore a different colored long tunic, reaching to the knees, over tight brown breeches. Woven belts wound their waists, the end straps hanging along the right thighs.

A wave of foreboding washed over her. Lilith took in each man in turn. The first walked with a slight limp, though it didn't detract from the power of his stance. Next a dark-haired knight with softer set features and an easier gait followed. His gaze moved over each of the women in interest.

Suddenly, Lilith's eyes stopped and her body froze. The third man in line towered the others in breadth and height. A raw, potent energy radiated from him, hitting her in the chest. Every nerve tingled with awareness and warmth, creating a curious reaction between her legs.

Lilith didn't know what to make of him. His size frightened her even as it intrigued her—so large and thick, yet so purposeful in his movements. He walked with a stalking grace that came only from years of exercise and training. Dark hair framed his face in thick waves, not so long as to touch his shoulders, but long enough to make her want to sink her hands into its depths and pull. Silken blue clung to the sculpted valleys of his chest and arms.

Then he looked at her, intense dark brown eyes piercing hers, and she couldn't breathe. He didn't smile, didn't show any pleasure in what he saw. The hard line of his mouth tightened, as if he wanted nothing more than to jump over the table and strangle her. Fists clenched alongside his thighs, tight, hard balls of steel that could easily take her head off with one blow.

Terror filled her. What had she done to draw his notice or his anger? Had she stared too long? Did he simply hate blondes? She wrapped her arms around her waist, hugging tight. The man wouldn't stop staring at her, as if he knew he dominated her with just that one look. Was he going to be her "first"?

"We have to get out of here," she whispered, filled with the urge to run.

"There is nowhere to go," Paige said, just as quietly. "I already tried. Resign yourself for we will never escape this place. Survive or die, those are your options."

Sorin took several deep breaths, feeling as he did when about to go into battle. Heat filled him as tension worked its way into his limbs. With a single thought, he could will his body to spring into action. He could erase her from the world and end this before it started.

But it was too late. He was lost the moment he'd looked at her, had seen her big blue eyes staring at him in trepidation. No, he was lost before that, when he *felt* her looking at him, beckoning him with her unwavering gaze to find her in the crowd.

Temptress. Witch.

He willed the desire inside him to go away. It shouldn't have been so strong. He'd relieved himself like he always did, had spilled his seed to ease the lonely ache.

Light from the fireplace shone through the white of her gown, silhouetting the long length of her legs and arms. The linen clung to her shoulders, swooping gently along the curves of her breasts— breasts that would be bare beneath. The tied hands were a new addition to the ceremony, thanks to Sir Aidan's wayward woman, Lady Paige. Sorin's barbaric side found he liked the addition.

Hunger rushed into every limb, lifting his cock beneath the long tunic. He didn't think to hide the reaction. No one would care. It had been so long, so very long, since he'd had a woman in his bed. He suppressed a groan. Soft flesh. Round breasts. Taut nipples. Slick, warm vessel to catch his passion. That certain female smell when he pressed his nose to her sex.

A thought whispered in the back of his mind. *Maybe she's different. Maybe she'll be better. Maybe this one will stay.*

He cursed the thought. No. She wasn't different. She wasn't better. Sorin had made up his mind long ago. He'd come, he'd look, but he never, ever wanted to find someone. He wasn't meant to have this, or her, or any kind of peace. Sorin was born into a land of war. He was made for it, every piece of him. One of the bloodiest battles in their history happened the very hour his mother gave birth to him.

Some were lucky to find peace in marriage, but not him. Tradition and necessity dictated he come to these ceremonies and try to find someone. He came from a noble line, a position of power, one that demanded he have sons to carry on his family's name. But society could not make him choose. It could not make him step forward and lay claim.

"Mine."

Where did that word come from? It sounded like his voice, booming over the hall to quiet all who watched into stunned silence. It felt like his body refusing to go to his place at the table, instead moving forward with arm uplifted to point at the blonde-haired beauty. But it couldn't be his body or his voice. That would mean he'd just announced his claim. Everyone would have heard it. He couldn't back out once the word was said.

"Sorin?" his younger brother, Ronen, hissed. Like Sorin, Ronen led one of the more renowned armies in all of Staria. Very few would dare to challenge their word or honor and the fact made it even more impossible for Sorin to take back what he'd done.

"Mine," Sorin found himself repeating. Was he possessed? What madness was this? He kept walking toward her. She merely stared at him, those wide, gorgeous eyes capturing his. Straight blonde hair hung long down her back, just as a woman's should.

"Brother?" Ronen questioned. The shock was evident in his voice. Sorin couldn't blame him for the surprise because that very day he'd been instructing Ronen to stay strong and not fall for a woman's pretty face. And what did Sorin do? He claimed a woman with a pretty face.

The hall remained quiet. Sorin stopped before the woman, noting with pleasure that she didn't cringe and fall away from his looming presence. Her strength would serve her well. Years of frustrated desires surged inside him. He couldn't put them off any longer. Deny it as he might, he needed a woman. He would never admit the words out loud. The need was not just for physical release, but for the softness of her, the sweet smell and the temporary relief from the endless fighting that such a creature could bring.

*You tried this before, Sorin. Such things are not for you.*

*Fool.*

*Idiot.*

*Weak.*

His accusing thoughts infuriated. Reaching for her bound arms, he took hold of the ropes. Not even his condescending inner voice could stop his actions. Sorin held her gaze steady, stating so she couldn't mistake his claim, "You are mine."

Did he say "mine"?

If she could have forced her limbs to move, Lilith would have blazed a trail out of there so fast the castle would've exploded. She'd heard about people being petrified with fear, but she never realized it felt like this. Not even her heart seemed to beat in her chest. She opened her mouth only to close it. Her eyes stared at his, unable to blink. Sound wouldn't leave her throat. She tried again, working her lips several times before managing a very inaudible, "No."

Dark eyes narrowed. This wasn't a man used to being refused. All around her, the hall had silenced. She heard the gasps as he'd first spoken, followed by rushed whispers. But none of the others could have been as stunned as she.

*This man wants me? This impossibly strong, muscular man? This deadly warrior with the imposing features and angry eyes?*

"Ah." The man standing near the head table cleared his throat. "Rejoice, Lord Sorin has chosen!"

The statement came out more like a question than an announcement. Cheering erupted, jarring Lilith to her senses. She jerked her bound hands, trying to free them. Lord Sorin held tight, unaffected by her protests.

"No," she managed, loud enough to be heard by the women standing next to her.

A low growl escaped Sorin.

"Stop it." Lilith tugged harder, not caring who heard. "Let me go. This is a mistake. I did nothing wrong. I'm not supposed to be here. Contact Divinity Headquarters on dimensional plane 269.

My employee number is 54367D. I don't belong here."

"Eh, my lord, if you wanted a woman, you should have waited to see their temperaments," a knight shouted, causing a round of laughter. "Methinks you found the shrew!"

"Ach, he's lucky to have a bit o' fire betwixt the sheets," another answered. A loud bang followed as people hit their goblets on the wooden tabletops.

"Are you saying my Bertha does not have fire?" the first man accused.

"Not as much as my Darla!" the second answered, the original playfulness no longer in his tone.

Fighting erupted behind her, but Lilith couldn't turn around. Sorin still stared at her, his dark eyes commanding.

"Come with me," Sorin ordered, tugging her behind him as he walked.

"Brother," the easy-going knight insisted from behind the table.

"It is done, Ronen," Sorin answered. "Tell Sera to send food to my chambers."

As he dragged her by her wrists from the crowded hall to a narrow archway next to the fire-place, Lilith tried to brace her feet against the floor.

The fruitless effort caused her to stumble erratically so she gave it up. She glanced behind her. The other women appeared a shade paler as they watched her being carted away like a newly acquired sex slave. And as far as she knew, that's exactly what she was.

## 3

LILITH TREMBLED as the giant man led her up a wide, spiraling stairwell. The noise of the hall faded behind her, insulated by the thick stone walls. The heavy thud of his boots echoed around her, encasing her in his ominous presence. He kept her wrists in his fist, but didn't look back at her.

She let her feet trip on the stairs, trying to make him stumble and let go. That's all she needed, for him to release her for just a second so she could run. Fleeing one man had to be better odds than fleeing from a packed hall. He didn't break stride, didn't let on that he felt her struggles. They passed a narrow slit in the wall, a thin window leading outside. They were getting high off the ground. She got a glimpse of an open field leading off into trees. Paige had told the truth.

"You have the wrong woman," Lilith broke the silence. Perhaps reason would work. Some primitive parallel cultures respected reasoning. "I'm an analyst."

Unexpectedly, he stopped and swung around to face her. "There is no mistake. The words were spoken, Lady Ann Anna List. It's done. You're mine."

She shook her head. He loomed over her, made all the taller by the higher step he stood upon. "I'm not—"

Sorin surged forward, tugging her into his chest at the same time. She crashed into him, gasping at the hard wall of his body. Not a measure of fat marred his thick frame. A shock of pure, sexual awareness poured over her flesh, enrapturing her nerves and turning her knees to weakened jelly.

"You are," he said.

"I'm not named Ann." Lilith's bound wrists were trapped between them, the sides pressed near the front of his thighs. If one of them moved, his cock would be squarely in her hands. "I-I'm Lilith Grian. I work for Divinity. Have you heard of them? I'm not supposed to be on this world. I'm not sanctioned to travel until after..." She paused, not wanting to say "my trial".

Sorin continued to stare at her, his brow slightly arched and his eyes cold.

"...after this thing. It's a mistake. Please, you appear very," she glanced at his chest, so close and powerful, "very reasonable. I'm sure you understand, I'm not—"

"You are," he answered, as if he hadn't heard a single thing she'd said.

Lilith gritted her teeth. Reason didn't work. Perhaps false bravado would. "I'm warning you. I'm trained to fight."

At that he grinned. The look did nothing to soften the hard lines of his face. He adjusted his hips and as she suspected, his cock pressed into her hands, letting her feel how very strong and powerful it really was. A hard knot formed in her stomach. Tears threatened her eyes as fear took hold. She held them back, feeling the burn in her nose. Her lips parted in shock and he took full advantage.

He didn't test her resolve or ask permission with a light brush of his lips. Instead, his mouth ordered her, commanding it to open wider with the probe of his tongue. The sweet, spicy taste of liquor flavored the hot kiss. It had been a very long time since a man kissed her like that.

Who the hell was she trying to fool? A man had never kissed her quite like that.

Pent-up desire and passion flowed through her, awakening nerves she'd long neglected. For a brief second, she thought of giving in. Who would know? This world was so far beyond the scope of hers. But when he had his way with her, would he pass her on to someone else? This man was a stranger on an uncharted world. She needed more facts. Lilith knew nothing about the true culture and laws of this place or of her place in it.

The taste of him burned into her mouth, combining with the very masculine smell of his body. She turned her head violently to the side, wrenching it back and forth to get her mouth away when his lips would follow. "No. Stop. Don't."

To her great surprise, Sorin let her go and stepped back. "You are right. This is not the place. Forgive me."

He hardly sounded contrite. Dizzy from the abrupt withdrawal, Lilith stumbled when he pulled her forward once more. The stone walls appeared to have darkened, not in reflected light but in color. "Where are you taking me?"

"The Black Tower," he answered, "our home. At least while we reside at Battlewar. When you come with me to the battlefront, we will stay in my tent."

"Our?" Lilith nearly collapsed in surprise. Did he just say she was going into battle? "Then you're not going to share me with the other men?"

"Share?" At that he almost looked offended. The blue tint of the stone faded into black, casting darker shadows over his face. Her heart raced and she backed away from the low tone of his voice. "I do not share what is mine. You are mine and you will not share yourself with others."

His possessive decree did not comfort her. Her breath sounded odd as it came out in rough pants. The end to this long stairwell had to be near.

"No, I'm not, Sorin," she said. "I don't belong here."

"You do now. I claimed you, you are mine. It is done. The decision is made." Coming to a door, he stopped and pushed it open. Without ceremony, he directed her inside.

Lilith's eyes went directly to the large bed covered with a fur pelt blanket. Firelight danced over the textured surface. She took a step away from him and then another, going the only direction she could —deeper into the chamber. The glint of metal caught her notice and she saw the weapons on the wall—gruesome, deadly instruments that would strike fear into anyone. The hilts were faded and worn, attesting to their frequent use.

Out of all the outcomes this day might bring, being tortured by deadly weapons hadn't crossed her mind. Lilith swallowed, realizing she'd held on to the idiotic idea that she'd be rescued if things went bad. But there was no safety feature hidden in her shapeless gown. Divinity would not be coming for her. This was real. Dark and twisted and real. If she refused, what would happen? If she gave in, what would he do? She'd never had a large warrior in her bed before, instead preferring to copulate with the tame, nonthreatening bookish types she met on assignment. There had been something safe and noncommittal to a man who lived on another plane—at least until now.

A warm hand touched the back of her neck and she gasped, jerking violently. She didn't dare move, but her eyes found a second door. It was only a few feet away, but it might as well have been a mile.

"Take this off," Sorin said. He brushed aside her hair and drew his mouth to her neck.

"Ah!" Lilith cried, running for the door. Her bound wrists made it impossible to pull the latch.

She couldn't do this. Not with him. Selfishly, she wished he'd chosen one of the others. Jayne seemed tough. She'd know what to do with a guy like this. Even the quieter Karre could have handled the giant before her better than Lilith ever could.

Her escape ended as fast as it began. Sorin grabbed her arm and spun her around. Her back hit against the hard wood of the door. Lilith inhaled a deep, shaky breath.

"I do not feel like playing a teasing game. There is much I have to do." He stroked her cheek and looked meaningfully to the bed.

"Please." Lilith looked at the weapon-filled wall, quivering so badly she could no longer stand on her own. "Please, don't hurt me."

SORIN WASN'T sure what exactly made him stop his pursuit. Her words were so soft and worried, and her body appeared so small and fragile trapped against the door. Her eyes stared at him in raw fear. He'd seen that look in battle—the wild, round gaze, the trepidation and terror. He did not want that look from her, not from the woman in his bed.

*Fool.*

*Idiot.*

*Weak.*

His body hummed with desire, reminding him how long it had been since he'd felt the softness of a female's touch. The painful arousal between his thighs annoyed him. Her resistance annoyed him. The wasted time he'd spend thinking about his new situation annoyed him. And the fact that he'd claimed her against all planning and better sense really annoyed him.

"Argh," he growled low in his throat. She jerked, closing her eyes tight. He could take her, make her want him. His desire begged him to. The taste of her mouth still lingered on his lips. She'd kissed him back in the stairwell. He'd felt her respond for the briefest of pleasurable seconds.

Why did she turn from him? Sorin didn't want her like this. He didn't want her scared of him, trembling like a fall leaf. Already he knew women were apprehensive of his size, but he was an accomplished lover. He could bring her to release. Even Bianka had given few complaints in that aspect of their marriage.

Sorin didn't need this aggravation. He needed someone who did her duty by him as he would by her. The Caniba tribes attacked further north than they ever had before, rising from the earth and disappearing like ghosts. That was where his concentration needed to be and he didn't have the time to explain it all to a stranger.

Frowning, he studied her tightly drawn face. He stepped back, pulling her away from the door so that he might open it. It had been a long time since he'd looked inside. The smell of dust wafted over him. Apparently, it had been a long time since any of the castle servants had gone in as well. It appeared they had listened to him when he ordered that the room should rot like the decay of his first marriage.

"You will live here," he instructed, feeling a slight twinge to think of another woman in Bianka's old quarters—even if Bianka only made use of it for one night. Light from his room cast into the dingy chamber, parting the shadows to reveal a dust-covered floor. Pale green cobwebs hung from the ceiling in withered strands, swinging gently and aimlessly. He hadn't thought to have the chamber prepared since he never planned on filling it. "Have it cleaned for it has seen little use. You should find whatever it is you females need for your daily routines."

"There's no other way out," Lilith observed, edging away from him. What happened to the proud woman who held her own in the main hall? He didn't like the protectiveness this fragile creature brought forth. "You're holding me prisoner?"

"There is no need to trap you, my lady. None of the others will touch you. They respect my claim." Sorin put distance between them. If she wasn't going to let him bed her, he wasn't sure what other need there was to be in her presence. His cock throbbed, so full and tight he could barely stand it. Every ounce of him pleaded for relief—the feel of her hand, the sucking kiss of her mouth, anything to end the suffering.

Striding to his fireplace, he grabbed an unlit torch and thrust it into the flames. Once lit, he went back into her room to find she hadn't moved. Sorin placed the torch in a sconce, casting the room with light.

He looked at the dirty bed. How easy it would be to bend her over the high edge. Growling low in his throat, he left her, slamming the door behind him. Once alone in his room, he paced the floor, tossing the front of his long tunic over his bent arm as he fumbled at the laces along his hip.

Sorin managed to free his sensitive cock from its painfully tight restraint. Every nerve in his body beseeched him to go to Lady Lilith. From the first moment, he wanted her. His body ached and his flesh burned.

"Witch," he whispered, trying to reason what had happened to make him claim her. "She's enraptured me in her spell."

He was lying to himself.

Starian men depended a lot on instinct. They made decisions fast and stuck by them. Sorin knew how to size up a person in a few seconds. In war, he had to know his opponent. Lilith held his most withering gaze when most men could not. She kept her arms close to her body when she moved and didn't wiggle and display herself for any man who cared to look in her direction. Her voice stayed soft, pleasingly so, even when she yelled. Well, "pleasingly" if he didn't take into account what she said. Hurt her? He'd never hurt a woman outside of battle, and then the heathen Caniba females could hardly be considered ladies on the same level as a Starian.

In one second, he knew. Lilith was for him. It did no good to deny it. He couldn't even explain it. But that was how their gods worked. He'd tried to force the ceremony before, thinking more of duty than fate. It had not worked out well for him. This time he acted on faith.

Then why in all of the burning forests was he standing alone in his bedchambers with his pants around his ankles about to grab his own cock?

Lilith caused his current affliction. It was her duty to take care of it. Why did she resist? The decision was made. She was his. Nothing would change that.

Gripping his erection hard, he began to stroke. This time, the vision of his new mistress filled his mind, fueling his passions. Sorin fell back onto his bed, into the soft fur of his coverlet. He cupped his balls, rolling them in his palm as he sought to bring himself relief.

LILITH PACED THE HORRIBLE BEDROOM, tugging at her bound wrists. A narrow window showed the impossible height of the tower she was supposed to call home. Even if she could squeeze through, it would be at least a nine-hundred-foot drop to her death. And falling was only a slightly worse option than going to face what awaited on the other side of the door.

Lord Sorin.

"Think, Lilith." She reached a dusty, spider-web-covered wall and turned to walk the other direction. This room was not acceptable. Sure, the amenities appeared to be fine, if she could dig them out from under the twenty thousand pounds of dust that covered almost every inch of the place. The only hint of the room's use before this night was a strange trail of footprints marring the blanket of dust on the floor. They started at Sorin's door and looked as though someone paced to the corner of the room, turned around and left, over and over again. "Forget the footprints. Forget the dust. Think, Lilith. Analyze the situation and come up with a plan. Academy might have been a long time ago, but you were trained to get out of sticky situations."

*Yeah,* her mind answered peevishly, *with the use of a Divinity emergency call-button hidden in my clothes.*

Now that she was out of Sorin's magnetically alluring presence, her mind seemed to come back from a foggy abyss. At the time, she hadn't realized the complete and utter effect he had on her. First, his eyes penetrated, causing every nerve to tingle. Then it was his smell, so masculine and erotic. He had the body of a gladiator, the grace of a martial artist and the face of a god of war. When he kissed her, raw passion washed across her body.

Lilith's breathing deepened and moisture pooled between her thighs. Each pacing step became a jolt to her system. She looked at the door. Who would know?

"I would," she answered her own question. "Think, Lilith."

Sorin's hands had been so strong and firm when they held her to the door, his tight body close to hers. And all he wanted was to throw her down on the bed and have his wicked, wicked way with her. With the way he moved and the very size of the rest of him, she just bet he knew how to work his well-endowed cock.

*Ah! Think of something else!*

"Um..." She looked around the room, desperate for a plan of escape. Just a few moments in Sorin's presence and she contemplated ways to separate him from his clothing. Men of war tended to have stamina. She bet he could last for hours.

*Stop it! I don't know anything about these kinds of men in bed. I'm no match for him. I don't like it rough, or painful, or... Stop it!*

He'd stopped when she'd told him to stop. Mr. Warrior Man had impulse control. Plus, he claimed no other man would touch her. He clearly was a man of power and, even if he wasn't, Lilith doubted any of the other knights would be stupid enough to cross such a formidable male.

"Escape." Lilith glanced at her bound wrists.

First things first, she needed her wrists free from the ropes. Unlike Sorin's room, hers didn't have a wall teeming with weaponry.

Lilith walked to the door and leaned her ear against the wood. Inside silence greeted her. After several seconds, she became relatively sure he'd left. Lilith fumbled at the latch before pulling it open. Sorin's bedroom seemed an odd contrast to her dirty one as she stepped over the dirt-lined threshold. Not a speck marred his floor or the immaculately polished blades on the wall.

Lilith began to lift her arms, intent on grabbing the nearest blade to free herself, when a very peculiar noise stopped her. Friction? Rubbing?

She turned to the bed and froze. Sorin lay on his back, his tunic pulled aside and his pants open. One strong hand pumped the length of his very erect cock. Lilith inhaled a deep, shaky breath. Her earlier assumption had been right. The man was extremely well-endowed. His eyes met hers, completely unconcerned with the fact she reached for one of his blades, and he didn't stop pleasuring himself.

"Ah," Lilith stammered. "Um?"

"Have you come to finish me?" His lids fell heavy over his eyes, but he kept them on her as he quickened his pace.

Lilith glanced at the wall. He thought she came to kill him? She must be a laughable opponent indeed if he didn't bother to look concerned.

"Good. I want you to finish me. Straddle my waist and—"

"Hands," Lilith managed, "going to get...for the hands."

Straddle him? Her heart hammered out of control.

"Take off your gown and come here," he ordered. "I desire you to finish me."

Lilith didn't know how to respond. Did the well-proportioned, godlike man have no shame?

"It is too close for me to stop, but I will recover quickly to finish you." He panted hoarsely.

*No, apparently not.*

His body tightened and she could sense he was close to release. A part of her wanted to obey, to at least finish watching the erotic display before her. Her sex tingled, aching to be filled by the incredibly giant cock in front of her. The size of him would undoubtedly hurt, yet she couldn't convince her pussy it didn't want to take every inch of his hard, thick arousal.

*Maybe a little pain and a little rough wouldn't be so bad.*

Images flashed in her mind, thoughts of straddling those tight, perfect hips. Or maybe she could crawl onto her hands and knees as he stood at the end of the bed, his bronzed body outlined by firelight as he thrust behind her. Then again, what would it be like to lie on her back and let him worship her with that beautiful mouth? Did strong manly men like him go down on their women?

"Come. Put your mouth on me and taste." He grunted heavily, his breathing harsh.

"Hands," Lilith answered a little too loudly before running through the open door to her bedroom. She hit the hard wood with her hands, slamming it shut.

Sorin heard the door close. A second later, he came, releasing his warm seed over his tight fist. He pumped a few more times, milking every last drop from his body.

Just seeing her face had been enough to thrust his desire to the breaking point. The pleasure of release mingled with disappointment. She'd watched him, her wide eyes taking in every stroke of his hand with obvious interest. Yet, she didn't act on what had to be a mutual lust.

Grumbling, he slid out of bed and righted his clothing. If Lilith wasn't going to do her duty, then he'd go back down and join the celebration. Despite the release, his mood soured quickly.

*She just watched and did nothing!*

Sorin stomped out of the room, taking the long row of steps two at a time. Coming quickly around a corner, he almost bumped into Sera on her way up with a large tray of food.

"Oh!" Sera gasped in surprise, awkwardly trying to curtsey under the weight of his glare. "My lord, excuse me."

Sorin growled at her, low and dark, nearly knocking her over as he quickened his pace. He needed a drink. Now.

"I TOLD you what you needed to do." Sera frowned as she sawed through Lilith's ropes. The serving women had tried untying them, but the men had bound the knots around her wrists too tight.

"Can you please hurry?" Lilith answered. "My fingers are numb."

"Your brain is numb," Sera insisted, sawing harder. The motion jiggled the serving woman's cleavage and Lilith looked away. "Keeping a happy bed is a simple enough task for the sake of the kingdom. I saw the look on his face. You did not do your duty by him."

"Easy, don't cut me!" Lilith jerked her arms when Sera sliced too close. She frowned on principal. "For your information, he did his own 'duty'. And I don't see what my sleeping with some overbearing lord has to do with the sake of the kingdom. If he wants to throw a temper tantrum, let him. It has nothing to do with me."

"Do you truly have no idea of by whom you have been chosen?" Sera asked, giving one last saw of the blade. The ropes fell free and Lilith moaned as she stretched her hands. Her fingers tingled sharply as blood rushed toward the tips. "Lord Sorin is one of the greatest warriors in the kingdom. It is a great honor to be his lover. None thought he'd ever claim a woman, not since his last one. It is your duty and honor to please him in all ways."

"Last one?" Lilith eyed the servant carefully. "What happened to the last one?"

"She did not please... Anyway, she's dead," Sera dismissed, clearly not wanting to get too far into it.

*Dead?!* Lilith gulped.

"Be Lord Sorin's vessel for release," Sera persisted. "Do not resist, do not deny and do not expect tenderness. In return, he will give you a noble life, my lady. Women would kill for the chance to be Lord Sorin's mate."

Lilith grimaced, reaching her arms over her head into a deep stretch. "I've heard this speech of yours before."

*Dead?!*

"Clearly, you did not or else you would have spread your thighs and drained the ill temper from him." Sera stood, huffing in irritation. She crossed to the tray of food she'd brought up with her and lifted it from a dressing table. "His mood affects the mood of his men, which in turn affects the moods of their women. Lord Sorin is not some lowly foot soldier. He's a hero."

"I don't care what you or the other women of this accursed dimension say." Lilith stood, facing the woman with her fists on her hips. Her hands ached but she ignored the discomfort. Even though she felt a very real attraction to Sorin, there was no way she could sleep with him. She refused on principal alone. "I am not and will not whore myself out to your precious Lord Sorin just because he is going to pout like a big baby who doesn't get his way."

"Well." Sera's mouth worked in anger. She set the tray down on the bed beside Lilith. The food slid around on the trencher and a small flurry of dust lifted around it. "I was going to order your bedchamber cleaned and gowns fitted, but now you can do it yourself, my lady."

Huffing, Sera marched out of the room, leaving Lilith alone.

Ignoring the tray on the bed, Lilith went to the pitcher Sera had put on the dressing table and poured herself a drink. The liquor burned, but she drank it gratefully. Under her breath she continued her fight with the now-absent servant, muttering, "Well, Sera, I've seen your outfit and I think I'll be better off if you didn't order my gowns for me."

## 4

Despite Sera's threat, two dozen maids arrived with buckets of hot water and fresh linens. Lilith watched in amazement as they made systematic work of the dirty room, scrubbing each stone and polishing each piece of furniture. A fire had been lit in the fireplace, casting a soft orange warmth over the interior.

The dark wood of the furniture gleamed in unsurpassed perfection. Simple engravings ringed the legs of the dressing table and matching chair. A cushioned seat rested near one wall paired with a small, circular table. For a society formed predominantly of warrior men, the slight delicateness of the furnishings surprised her.

Out of all the objects, she found the four-poster bed the most extravagant. The same rings wrapped the legs, matching it to the dressing table set. The dingy comforter was replaced with a richly embroidered red and gold. Lilith already knew from sitting on the mattress that it had been designed for comfort. Suddenly, the image of Sorin on his back, pleasuring himself, came to mind and she quickly looked away. Just thinking of his rock-hard body moving with warlike grace made her shiver.

She had to get out of Staria. Fast.

The servants nudged her out of their way, not deigning to speak to her as they whispered amongst themselves. She curled her toes against the damp stone beneath her feet, really missing her own clothes. Even though they ignored her, she didn't dare leave the tower for risk of facing Sorin and more angry Battlewar citizens. Thoughts of what Sera said filled her mind, not so much the "please him or he'll be in a bad mood" part, but the last woman he'd been with ending up dead.

Did Sorin kill his last lover for not pleasing him? She saw the danger in his gaze, the simmering emotions just below his hot surface. Would he kill her if she didn't sleep with him? And what if she slept with him but wasn't any good at it? How could she tell if she was any good at it? Would she be good at it if she was nervous about being good at it?

Lilith's stomach tightened and she felt as if she might be sick. She needed to think of something else, *anything* else. Eyeing a nearby maid, she said, "Excuse me, but what is philter? The guards said they were giving it to some of the women. Is it a poison?"

The woman waved a dismissing hand. "It's to make you forget things."

"So the other women, they weren't killed?" she insisted. The servants all stopped what they were doing to look at her in offense.

"The otherworlders were sent home," the maid ground out and they all went back to work with a renewed fury. Under her breath, the woman muttered, "They weren't suitable for this world." By the glance she gave Lilith, it became clear she didn't think her suitable either.

As the last of the withered cobwebs were wiped away, all but two of the women left the room. Placing their hands on the stone wall perpendicular the door, they pushed. Lilith watched in amazement as the women moved the wall. Stone scraped against stone and light streamed in from within the hidden room.

"What is it?" Lilith couldn't help her curiosity.

"Your bath, my lady," a giggly brunette named Nan answered. A row of stone steps led up to an inset tub, large enough to fit five of her comfortably. The servant stepped inside the tub and twisted a metal ring on the bottom to tighten the plug. Fresh air flowed from several narrow slits in the wall, giving a slight chill to the air.

"Unless you prefer a metal tub like my lord," Hannah added, her big green eyes looking more at the floor than directly at Lilith. Her bright red hair was piled high on her head.

"This is fine," Lilith said, a little uncomfortable with the way they spoke to her. She was used to fading into the background, not being treated like a princess about to give royal decree—albeit a despised princess being blamed for the ill fate of the entire kingdom.

"Yea, my lady." Hannah went to a hand pump and began to work the lever up and down, filling the bath with blue-tinted water. Nan climbed out of the tub, narrowly missing getting her shoes wet. To Lilith's surprise, steam rose around them. The water was heated.

Nan must have seen Lilith's amazement because she giggled and explained, "The blue minerals in the natural underground springs keep the water warm."

"Interesting," Lilith said more to herself as she reached to touch the water. Sapphire-blue droplets dripped off her fingertips. "I haven't seen this before on the other planes."

"Do you need assistance, my lady?" Nan asked.

"No," Lilith rushed. "I can do it myself."

The two women bowed and shuffled out of the bedrooms. The sound of their laughter could be heard, fading into the distance.

Lilith contemplated the water, wondering if it would stain her skin to an unnatural color. Then, deciding at this point she didn't care, she shrugged out of her shapeless gown and stepped into the bath.

*Did Sera really mean to say dead?*

SORIN'S COCK STILL ACHED. The desire he'd managed to keep at bay all these years flared its randy head now that it had a target. And what a lovely target she was, too. He longed to touch her pliant flesh, flesh that would mold to his will, and her velvety soft hair and even softer lips.

What in all the bloody battles happened? One look at a woman and suddenly a hole as wide as the castle punctured his neat and orderly world. As if his fate wasn't bad enough, his brother, Ronen, had also claimed a woman. What sort of witchery beset them this day? Two of the most confirmed bachelors in the land were now bound.

They'd been fools to enter into this agreement for women. When Divinity first approached them in the midst of battle, the Starians had almost slaughtered them where they stood, believing the oddly dressed creatures to be allies to the Caniba tribes. After much negotiation, investigation, a little bit of pleading by the Divinity scouts, and hours of council meetings, an alliance was formed with the alien beings.

Divinity wished for samples of the blue mineral water, water that stayed warm no matter how long it sat away from another heat source. The blue water springs ran deep and wide. There was no shortage of the mineral and giving some away was a little enough consideration. In return, the Divinity aliens provided a resource much needed by the Starians—women. Out of the women Divinity sent, three were chosen as being of the right temperaments to stay. The new blood was just one of the reasons all the "firsts" were of high military rank or distinction.

"Ronen, you fool," Sorin muttered, lifting a goblet to drink deeply. He stared at the woven banners along the wall, each depicting an important Starian religious and political symbol.

"I could well blame you, brother," Ronen

answered, brooding next to him. None in the hall dared to break their dark mood. "You fell first. I had no choice."

A darkening bruise marred Ronen's cheek where his woman had struck him, and his clothes, though on, were exceedingly disheveled. At least his brother's woman fought him. Lilith cowered like she thought he might run her through with a blade.

Sorin growled low in the back of his throat. Curious eyes turned toward them from the hall floor, but none dared to approach. "I did not fall. These foreign women have bewitching powers. We should never have entered into an agreement with the otherworlders."

Ronen grumbled incoherently.

Eager for a more comfortable subject, Sorin turned his attention to Sir Rian. The knight had stood next to them during the ceremony as a first, but had luckily chosen no woman. If he had, he'd not be drinking with his fellow knights. Waving the soldier to the head table, he gestured that the man should sit. Rian didn't hesitate, despite the forbidding moods of the brothers, and took a seat next to Sorin. "Any word from Lord Serik's man? Do the Caniba armies march against the forces at Spearhead?"

"They do not march yet, but Lord Martin

suspects it will be soon," Rian answered, keeping his tone low. "Sorceress Magda's scouts were captured in the southern marshes, but at the loss of two good men —Richard of Daggerpoint and Peeter of Fallenrock. They died well and were not taken by those cannibals. Sir Vidar goes to lead the interrogations. He has already left with his new bride."

"Vidar, too?" Ronen sighed before muttering again to himself. Sorin frowned, sorry for his friend's shared misfortune.

"Yea, Vidar, as well," Rian agreed. "Though he looked about as pleased as the two of..." The words tapered off and Rian gave the brothers a dismissing wave of his hand.

"And Aidan?" Sorin asked. All knew without question that the last woman, the infamous Lady Paige who'd been a gift from the fairies, would go home with her husband, Sir Aidan. "How did he fair?

"He did not look well when he left Battlewar." Rian leaned forward to grab an abandoned goblet and lifted it to a maid. She nodded, running to fetch him a clean one. "Nor did Lady Paige."

"This is a bad year for finding mates," Ronen asserted, his frown deepening. "Perhaps we should cancel the ceremonies, especially those involving the otherworlders."

"The decisions are made," Sorin broke in, knowing honor would not let them change their minds. He reached his goblet out as a maid appeared with a pitcher. He already felt the heady effects of the drink but didn't care. Right now he wanted to feel numb. Maybe liquor could take the terrible ache in his loins away. "There is no reason to contemplate them."

"Though, it does not mean we have to choose the women they send," Rian offered.

Sorin focused his attention on his brother. Ronen leaned to the side to address Rian. "What other news?"

"Not much else. Lines hold strong on both sides. Vidar hopes to discover where the Sorceress' encampment lies. We suspect she is in the Hanging Forest, but..." Rian didn't reveal anything they didn't already know. One of the self-proclaimed queens of the Caniba tribes, Sorceress Magda was as elusive as she was cruel. Over the last four years, she'd been one of the more aggressive Caniba factions attacking the borders.

"We should ride to the borderlands," Ronen said,

drawing Sorin's wandering attentions back to the conversation. "We will be of more use there."

"We have not been summoned," Sorin lowered his voice to a whisper, "and unless the king orders otherwise, we will be forced to bring the women with us."

"Not if they become with child," Ronen reasoned.

Sorin tensed, reminded of how unlikely that possibility was at the moment. The accursed woman rejected him. Him!

How proud it would make him to have a child, whether it be a boy or girl. However, admittedly, his aim when it came to Lady Lilith wasn't so noble as perpetuating the family line. He wanted a lover first and a wife second. "We would do better to pray for war, brother."

DEAD.

The word wouldn't leave her, no matter how hard Lilith tried to erase Sera's comment. The idea that a woman, a sex slave, would be killed for not performing wasn't totally unheard of in the histories of the parallel worlds. Staria was clearly a barbaric land, from their simple "mine" ceremony to the "lord and lady" structure of their undoubtedly feudal society. In what most places remembered as the medieval period, lords often took what they wanted with little effective protest from the masses. If Lord Sorin wanted her, she doubted any would stop him. None had tried so far and none had reason to do so.

And if Lord Sorin wanted her dead?

Lilith trembled, missing the safety of an old library and dusty books as she studied and recorded historical facts. By the time she got there, her assigned dimension had been cleared by a tactical team, usually several of them, and was deemed safe.

"I have to act," she determined. "Survival first."

Coming up with a plan was easier than implementing it. The maids had left behind a thin linen cloth for drying after her bath. As she wandered the room, looking for her white gown, she realized that the linen was all they had left her.

"Sera," Lilith muttered accusingly. The servant probably thought she'd be helping Lord Sorin by stealing his sex slave's clothes.

After digging through every drawer and small trunk in her room to no avail, Lilith decided to check Sorin's. She couldn't very well wear the bed sheet or the fur coverlet downstairs. Wet hair stuck to the back of her neck as she slowly opened the door to Sorin's room. All was silent, but she peeked in at the bed anyway. He wasn't there. Disappointment filled her and she wondered at it.

*Put your mouth on me and taste.*

Part of her had wanted to do just that, but fear held her back.

"Be brave," Lilith whispered, stepping into the empty chamber. She went first to his trunk at the end of his bed and pulled back the lid. Neatly stacked clothes lined one side and pieces of armor filled the other. Lifting a black tunic with a red patch on the chest, she brought it to her nose. It almost smelled like him, clean and fresh, but lacking that very masculine quality.

Not wanting to dig through his things, she decided the long tunic would work. She fitted it over her head, taking the first belt she saw to tie the waist like a dress. The shirt fell to her calves and bunched at the shoulders. She rolled the sleeves so her hands poked out of the bottom.

With bare feet, she made her way from the room and down the tower steps. She took them two at a time. Confusion warred inside her and she doubted what she was about to do.

*Curse it! I need facts. How can anyone make a decision without all the facts?*

Her feet padded on the stone, making soft, steady noises as she quickened her pace. Then, seeing the end of her journey down the steps, she slowed. The sound of voices carried in from the main hall where the knights gathered. In the opposite direction, she heard the clang of metal and smelled the distinct aroma of baking bread.

"Hey!" the whispered hush caused Lilith to jolt in alarm. A hand slipped over her mouth and pulled her to the side. Jayne appeared next to her, pressing close as they hid inside a narrow alcove behind the tower stairwell. Glancing down, Jayne chuckled, "Looks like we shop at the same store."

As the woman let go of her mouth, Lilith looked at Jayne's clothes. She wore the exact same tunic, only Jayne had cut her sleeves to length instead of rolling them. Her hair had been pulled back into a single ponytail at the back of her head, tied with what seemed to be the excess sleeve material.

"I overheard the maids talking," Jayne said. "I was about to come up to the tower to get you." She looked at Lilith's bare feet. "Couldn't find any shoes to steal? Follow me, there's a laundry room this way. They have shoes."

Lilith didn't know what to say to her. Jayne stared at her with pity and determination, but there was something else behind her gaze—fear. What had happened to her to make her look like that? Though smoothed back, her hair had a disheveled appearance to it. Had the men hurt her? Had she been claimed by someone with less self-control than Sorin? Lilith tried to think of the right thing to say to comfort the poor woman, but couldn't come up with the right words.

Jayne leaned forward and kept her voice low. She tugged on Lilith's arm. "Come with me. I promise Lord Sorin won't touch you again, but you have to make a fight of it."

"Wait." Lilith refused to move. Jayne's words confirmed her suspicions. Something terrible had happened to the woman. "What did they do to you? Did they hurt you?"

Jayne glanced everywhere but at Lilith's direct gaze. "No, they didn't touch me, but I don't want to give them the chance to."

"What are you planning to do?"

"Karre and Paige have been taken south by a couple of the barbarians. With any luck, we'll be able to find them. Paige seems to know her way around this backwater place." Jayne again tried to pull her. "The timing is perfect. They're in there having a party and getting drunk. It will be dark soon. We'll find a way out of the castle and wait until nightfall. If we travel by dark, we should make it through the prairie to the forest. From there, by the grace of some miracle, we'll find a trail to follow—"

"You're going to escape?" Lilith jerked Jayne back. She might not have known the woman all that long, but she was really the only friend Lilith had in the castle. Mutual circumstances made for a joint cause. "You can't, Jayne. I've talked to a few of the servants. If we displease them, I think they might kill us."

"They didn't kill Paige for running," Jayne reasoned.

"Yet," Lilith asserted. "How do you know that's not what they're taking her south for? You heard the guard. Her master might delve out a harsh punishment."

Jayne paled. "What would you have us do? We can't stay here forever, waiting for them to get tired of us. What if they try to philter us like the others— whatever that means. What if they make us take on more men? If you saw what I saw walking these hall- ways, you'd know we have to run. I can't stay here and be a whore and that's exactly what I think this place is. A whorehouse."

A whorehouse? Lilith wasn't so sure. "I was told the philter is a drug to make you forget you've been here. They said those women from the cell with us were sent home because they were unsuitable."

"I don't think that'll work for us. We've been chosen to stay." Jayne didn't make it sound like much of an honor. If she thought this place was a brothel, Lilith could understand why.

"I think we should stay in the castle for now. Sorin didn't seem too keen on passing me around to all the men." Lilith reached caringly toward her. "Are you sure you weren't hurt? Did your man...? Did he make you...?"

"Ronen? No. He didn't try to pass me out." Jayne shook her head in denial. "I would have ripped off his balls had he tried."

"I can learn more here in civilization than in the woods. If we keep our heads low and try to behave, maybe we'll find a way home. I think we'll have better luck here at a castle than in the wild. Besides, running is too big of a gamble. How will we survive in the wilderness? How will we eat? What kind of animals are in the forest? Poisons? Flora and fauna? Insects? What about the people the Starians are fighting? What's out there could be much, much worse than what is in here. Paige seemed really scared when she spoke of the monsters."

"Paige could be lying. This castle could be a theme place and beyond the compound is a thriving society with technological advances. Whatever it is, I can't stay here. I'm not scared of dying," Jayne stated grimly, "but I will never live as some man's slave. Please come with me."

Lilith looked to the main hall. The unknown outside these castle walls or Lord Sorin's property? With one she'd have freedom. With the other she'd have shelter, food, protection and access to the castle grounds to look for a way home.

"I can't go with you," Lilith decided. "I'm taking my chances here."

"Do you have a plan?"

Lilith nodded, trying to look confident. "I think so. If I find a way to escape, I'll do my best to let you know about it."

"And if I do, I'll try to send word," Jayne glanced down and smiled, "in a pair of shoes."

"Good luck to you then." Lilith held out her hand.

"And to you. Don't let them break you. One way or another, we're going home. I promise." Jayne shook it briefly before disappearing down the hall the way she'd come.

Lilith watched after Jayne feeling very alone. All her prison buddies were gone, leaving her at the castle. She felt confident in her decision to stay and only wished Jayne would have remained as well. Traipsing across foreign countryside wasn't a logical plan of action, no matter how badly she wanted to run away from the powerful Lord Sorin. Still, she respected Jayne for taking the risk.

Lilith turned her attention to the main hall, trying to build up her nerve. She couldn't do this, even if just thinking of him made her entire body tingle. Sorin was too big, kissed with so much aggression. Of course, with him being the aggressor, she wouldn't have to do much by way of seduction.

*Be Lord Sorin's vessel for release, do not resist, do not deny...spread your thighs and drain the ill temper from him.*

As arousing as the idea was in the theoretical, Lilith was frightened by the idea of the actual. Sure, the thought of Sorin would fuel any woman's late night fantasies. Who wouldn't be attracted to a big warrior man with alpha tendencies and the body of sheer perfection? Even now she felt the impression of his large cock against her stomach. The man had been trained to move and knew his body.

"If his displeasure doesn't kill me, his body just might." Lilith took a deep, shaky breath. "By all the gods worshiped in all the parallel universes, please don't make me regret this."

## 5

SORIN STOPPED LISTENING to his brother as all senses went on alert. Ronen didn't talk about anything important, just words to add fuel to their mutual drunkenness and gloom. Normally, if they were upset, they'd volunteer to ride out and face the enemy whether the enemy engaged them or not. There was nothing like a hard and vicious fight to drive the demons away. But because of their idiotic decisions, they couldn't even find the sanctuary of battle to leave them in exhaustion. No, instead they were stuck at Battlewar with seductresses sent to torment them.

"...pray for an attack..." Ronen was saying. Sorin nodded in agreement, not hearing the whole statement.

His skin tingled and the nerves pulled his attention toward the hall floor. Instinct told him Lady Lilith had to be near. Jealousy and mistrust caused his eyes to scan the main hall floor, searching every knight, every filled lap and busy pair of arms.

"...it is better to die in battle than..." his brother continued.

*I'll kill the wench before I let another woman embarrass me again*, Sorin swore. *I will not be cuckolded. I will not be dishonored.*

Bianka's faithlessness had been a huge blow to his masculine pride and reputation. His honor would not recover a second time.

Sorin's vision blurred slightly, as his gaze traveled once more over the main hall. It had been a long while since he'd drank to such excess. Seeing blonde hair, he stiffened, ready to pounce. The woman straddled Gregor's lap, wiggling brazenly as she kissed his neck. The man pulled on the blonde waves, jerking her face toward the ceiling. Sorin blinked hard, bringing her into sharp focus.

"Margaret," he muttered. The blonde was Gregor's wife.

"What of her?" Ronen inquired.

"What of who?" Sorin pretended not to understand.

"Margaret?" Ronen persisted.

"What of Margaret?" Sorin grumbled.

"I thought..." Ronen's words tapered off. "Never you mind. I'm drunk and hearing voices. The woman has ridden me mad."

There. Lilith.

Sorin caught his breath. He'd found her. Lilith waited in the doorway, watching the hall with a mixture of trepidation and determination. She gripped the stone, her body hidden from view—all but her lovely face, a black covered arm and one bare foot. Her eyes darted to his briefly before looking to the floor. Her foot pulled back, as if she would hide.

Sorin held still, watching to see what she'd do. Wide blue eyes captured his once more, looking nothing like the near black pits of Bianka's soulless gaze. From the very beginning, Bianka had an air to her. She charmed everyone, being exactly what they wanted her to be. Well, at least at first she had. All Sorin had wanted was a mate, someone to share life's journey with. Bianka had never been that.

His heartbeat quickened and he gripped the stem of his goblet tight. Was he mistaken or did Lilith try to smile at him? Her lips parted, drawing his full attention, and her fingers curled as if to call him toward her. Liquid heat swirled inside him, blazing down his chest to lift his cock in thick arousal. He forgot the hall and his chatty brother. Thoughts raced, but the hesitance of his mind didn't stop his body.

Sorin stood, leaving his goblet on the table. The cup was empty anyway. The more he consumed, the longer it took the maids to refill his drink. Or perhaps, he simply drank faster. It didn't matter now, with her standing there, staring at him, and beckoning him with her very presence.

Lilith stiffened, coming more into view as she faced him. He half expected her to run, but she held firm. Did she know how she affected him? Surely women were born with such knowledge. She had to know that licking her bottom lip only made him look at it with longing. She had to know that her eyes, wide and beautiful and clear, caused his chest to tighten with the urge to hold her against him and protect her from all things. Her loose hair made his fingers flex to run the entire silky length.

What was it about women that could make men fall to their knees and forget everything?

*Fool.*

*Idiot.*

*Weak.*

Only when he neared did he take note of her

clothes. The dark red of his family crest stared out at him, branding her as his. She'd grabbed his battle tunic, the shirt he wore when he led men to war. It identified him as a leader, and her wearing it only publically declared she thought herself above him. Sorin glanced behind him, wondering if anyone else saw. A few of the knights frowned in her direction, shaking their heads.

"My lord," she said, her voice trembling.

Sorin grabbed her arm and pulled her out of the archway before anyone else noticed her clothes. "What are you doing, Lady Lilith?"

"I came down to..." She motioned weakly to the stairway, then to the hall. Her gestures made no logical sense. He let go of her arm, crossing his over his chest. She pulled back from him as he towered menacingly over her.

"What is the meaning of this?" He pointed at his tunic.

"I..." She looked down her body. "The servants..."

By all the bloody sword blades, if she didn't look sexy in his clothes!

"The maids took mine and I didn't have anything to wear and I wanted to come down here and..." She picked at the coat of arms on her chest, flicking the edge of the embroidery with her fingernail.

"And?" he prompted, aware of how hard he sounded.

"And," she repeated.

"Well?" He shifted his weight from one foot to the other, placing his hands on his hips.

"This." Lilith shot forward, arms rising toward his head. She brought her face quickly forward.

Sorin automatically defended himself, easily capturing her wrists and jerking them to the side. Her body slammed into his chest. When he looked at her face, her eyes were closed and her lips were puckered, as if she'd been about to kiss him. Her forehead bumped into his chin, knocking hard.

She made a small noise of pain. Lilith's eyes opened in shock at his rough hold and her lips pulled tight against her teeth. "Oh, I, ah, I'm not any good at... Okay, sorry, you can let me go now. Go back to drinking. Forget I came down."

She struggled to pull her hands free. Sorin tightened his grip. Without hesitating, he swooped in for a kiss. His lips met hers. She gasped and he took it as an invitation for more. Who was he to turn down such sweetness? Mindlessly he kissed her, delving his tongue into the very depths of her mouth.

Sorin let go of her wrists, only to wind his hands along the small of her back to hold her closer. The tunic slid beneath his touch, revealing a smooth texture underneath. She wore no undergarments to hamper his discovery. He rocked his hips, reveling in the pressing heat of her stomach. His cock ached, urging him on. With the way he felt, he could love her all night and all morning. Hard, soft, fast, slow, he didn't care how or where. He burned to be inside her.

Lilith lifted her hand to touch his jaw, sending light, feathery caresses across his cheek. The willing exploration threw brush on the dangerous inferno of his greedy passions. His kisses became aggressive as he nipped at her mouth, drawing her bottom lip between his teeth.

She made a weak noise and twisted her head to the side. The sound of her ragged breath beat against his ear. Sorin kept kissing, devouring her jaw and neck, nipping and licking wherever his mouth could reach. The feverish rhythm of her pulse drummed along his lips. She felt it too, this deep passion, she had to.

She tasted like honey and sweet berries. His hands worked along her back, urging the tunic up. Sorin groaned, not caring who heard him. The people of Staria were not shy about their passions.

Why should they be? Having sex was as natural as breathing and infinitely more fun than war.

"Not here," she breathed heavily into his neck. "Please, not here. I can't if..."

Her words caused him to look around. His cock screamed in protest, declaring that here and now was perfect. Almost confused, he looked for a place to take her. The wall? The stairwell? The floor?

"I can't in front of the others. Please, don't make me. I don't want them watching." She shivered in his arms, glancing meaningfully at the main hall. Sorin studied her face, done in by the way she bit her lip.

*Anything my lady desires of me.*

Sorin stiffened. The thought wasn't like him. He was not a man to bend to the will of others. "Where would you have me take you?"

*Fool.*

*Idiot.*

*Weak.*

"May we go back upstairs?" She said the words, but her eyes didn't look as certain. He wondered at the change in her, but didn't ask. Her lush lips reeled him in and he captured them with his own. Moaning, he lifted her off the floor, letting her feet dangle as he carried her upright toward the stairwell of the Black Tower.

Her legs swayed and the natural rocking of her body hit against his already strained cock. Traveling up would be torture, but he was loath to put her down. Sorin pulled her closer, wishing she'd wrap her legs around his waist.

Lilith held on to his shoulders, gripping tight. He kissed her harder. She moved her lips, but her tongue didn't delve into his mouth. He sucked, trying to draw it forward to explore and taste.

Soft globes rubbed his chest through the material of their clothes. He needed to feel them. Quickening his pace, he carried her up the tower stairs. Her grip tightened, her legs pulling strangely to the sides as if looking for hold on the stone walls.

Nearing the halfway point, he stopped. Her nearness was agony. He couldn't wait. Later he would take her in a bed, but for now the privacy of the stairs would have to do.

Lilith's feet hit the floor and she swayed weakly, her knees giving out before she could catch herself. Sorin held her arm, keeping her from falling. "No one will happen upon us here, my lady."

*Here?*

Lilith gulped. Already she knew she had made a grave mistake in going to him. She was out of her league. At least in a bed she knew she'd had a little practice to back up her meager skills as a lover.

Sorin's intensity frightened her. Just the size of him, without the piercing force of his dark brown eyes, made her quiver. But when he stared at her, with the unmistakable look of a predator about to devour prey, she nearly fainted.

Sorin leaned in to her and Lilith leaned away. He stalked her until she sat on a step, perched along the uncomfortable ledge. How in the world did he plan on making this work? He braced an arm beside her, trapping her beneath with little air separating their bodies.

Sorin reached for her, touching her hair. The dark tan of his flesh contrasted the blonde. He fingered the strands, gripping them so that the roots pulled slightly. It didn't hurt, but she wondered at the greedy way he licked his lips.

The waves of his hair framed his face. Now that she could see him in finer detail, she noticed the scars that ran along his neck. One began at an ear and sliced down, just missing a vital artery. Another started at the base of his throat and disappeared beneath the neckline of his tunic.

Her breath caught, a phenomenon that seemed to happen a lot when she was around him. His hand left her hair for her chin, continuing downward, over her neck to glide over the material of her borrowed tunic.

To her surprise, when he reached a breast, his touch turned caressing and gentle. A light moan left his parted lips. A trail worked down her breast to the blazing heat of her sex. If he kept touching her like that, she wouldn't be able to control herself.

Lilith tilted her head back, closing her eyes. But as suddenly as the slow seduction started, it ended. Sorin's hand became firm, squeezing harder before letting go to unfasten her belt. A leg bumped into hers, and she opened her eyes to find him fumbling with the laces to his pants. He'd pulled his tunic aside, which revealed the unmistakable strength of his arousal beneath the barrier of clothing.

Harsh pants of air washed over her, zealous in Sorin's eagerness. Unsure of what to do, she began to back away. This wasn't what she imagined. The whole scene had been planned out in her mind. She'd go down and get him to come back up. She'd "please" him—in a bed—so he wouldn't be tempted to kill her. Then that would be that. Nowhere did her plan allow for passion-induced, near-crazed warrior man with a formidable weapon taking her on the uncomfortable stairwell with people milling just feet away.

"Pull up your skirts," Sorin ordered, his voice hoarse.

Lilith acted on instinct. Though every nerve inside her pussy yelled and screamed for him to touch it. Her confused, out-of-depth mind revolted. She needed to regroup and come up with a new plan. Oh, why hadn't she run away with Jayne?

*Run away. Good plan.*

Lilith turned, intent on running up the stairs until she could get her overheated body under control. Sorin's nearness only caused confusion and chaos. When he kissed her, she couldn't think straight. If she couldn't think straight, how was she to make sure she was any good in bed and thus avoid the whole "dead" scenario?

"Mm, yea, my clever lady," Sorin groaned in approval. He grabbed her hips before she could fully stand. Now her back was to him and she couldn't see what he was doing. "It will be easier to take you like this."

Lilith's fingers worked against the rough texture of the stone. His warm hand slid up her leg, boldly moving up her outer thigh. Emotions waged a confused battle over her. She wanted him. She'd just met him. It felt really good when he touched her like that. This wasn't logical or considered. This had to stop. She needed to think. What was she doing here? One little mistake on the job would not warrant banishment. But if it did? What would she do? What if she couldn't find a way home? And did he have to grab her ass like that?

The cool air of the stairwell hit her flesh as he bared her from behind. Lilith made a weak noise, the sound somewhere between panic and pleasure. Callused hands, strong and sure, explored at will. Fingers ran up her spine and down her ribs, teasing the sides of her breasts.

The bittersweet ache of his touch filled her, concentrating every part of her being on the needy ache in her sex. She closed her eyes tight, remembering the size of him, how rough he could be when he kissed her, held her. He touched her pussy and she jerked, knowing he found the betraying wetness of her arousal. A low, dangerous groan left him, loud and echoing against the stone.

Lilith opened her mouth to speak, unsure whether the words would be a protest or approval. His cock had been as large as him as she'd watched him pleasure himself. How did they get like this? She couldn't see his eyes. She wanted to see his eyes. What was he thinking? What was he looking at? What was he...?

And then it happened—an incredibly thick pressure, entering, probing. She couldn't help herself as she yelped in surprise, jerking away from him before his cock made it more than a half inch past the entrance. Lilith reached for the next step, ready to scurry away and regroup. Sorin's hold on her hips stopped her.

He brushed her again, his cock glancing along her inner thigh. Lilith tensed.

*I want this. I can't want this. I want this. I can't want this. Oh please, don't hurt me.*

For a long time his fingers worked, clenching and unclenching against her hips. She stayed rigid, waiting, anticipating, over-thinking every second. Her hand clutched the step, working violently into the hard stone.

"You act as if you don't want this." Sorin's words were low, harsh and unmistakably upset.

"No," she answered, trying to form a complete thought.

"No? Then why did you beckon me to you? Why did you summon me from the hall and put your lips to mine?" His grip tightened, painful now.

"Please," she begged. "I don't want to die."

"Die?" This time he let go. Without his support, Lilith fell against the steps. All too aware of her naked ass hanging out for him to see, she pushed frantically at her clothes to cover it. "Did the Divinity leaders tell you they would kill you if you didn't come here?"

"They didn't say anything," she answered, unsure if she should be pleased he finally seemed to listen to her about her erroneous presence.

"Then why would you die?" Sorin wasn't so modest as to cover himself. His pants clung to his large thighs, held up only by the sheer breadth of his muscles. The tunic had been pushed aside, catching now on the incredibly erect length of his cock.

"Because if I don't please you, you'll kill me like your last lover," she blurted, instantly wishing she could take it back.

Sorin's eyes darkened as he narrowed them in rage. A ripple washed over him, stiffening every muscle. Lilith cowered on the steps, trying to press her body into them until she faded into the hard stone. His chest rose and fell, panting heavily, and his fists clenched at his sides as if any second he could tear her apart.

"Who told you of Bianka?" he demanded.

Lilith shivered violently, managing a small shake of her head. No words would come out of her mouth.

"Argh!" He slammed his hand into the wall, and she screamed. Lilith backed away from him, knowing that the tower would only trap her, but unwilling to try to push past him. When he didn't stop her, she turned and ran, stumbling as her legs tangled in the skirt of her tunic.

Reaching his bedchamber door, she pushed inside and slammed it shut, not stopping until she was blockaded inside her new room with the vanity pushed tight against the door. Light from the open bathroom wall shone over the room, helping her to see as she made her way over to burrow under the covers. Turning her eyes to watch the bedroom door, Lilith doubted the barricade would keep him out if he wanted to get in, but the furniture line of defense gave her a small measure of comfort.

SORIN GLARED AT HIS ERECTION, hating that he still wanted Lady Lilith even after her words. A tiny voice whispered to take her anyway, to not stop. It was his right, after all. He couldn't. He was not the monster she thought him to be.

How did she know about Bianka or her death? Apparently, the servants gossiped and the fact only served to fuel his rage. He had ordered all talk of his late wife to cease. If he could have, he would have ordered all thoughts of her erased from the minds of Starian society.

How dare Lilith come to him like that? How dare she kiss him, let him kiss her? And how dare she show him her perfect ass, so smooth and unflawed, so unlike the hard scar-riddled length of his body. But, most of all, how dare she give him a glimpse of happiness only to rip it away?

Sorin braced his hand on the wall and gripped his cock hard, pouring all his anger into the yanking thrusts of his tight fist. She didn't want him. That much was clear. She only came to him because she thought he'd kill her if she didn't. Death or his bed? Those were the choices she believed she had?

And kill her? Kill her?! What was he? A dishonorable brute? A mindless Caniba? A beast who raped and pillaged? The insult cut deeply into his pride. Why did the gods of war curse him? He did all they demanded of him. He went into battle without hesitancy. He lived by the sword.

Sorin found no pleasure in the act of release, only a bitterness that was hard to contain. His seed spilled onto the steps but he didn't care. Twice he'd been cursed. The first was a cuckolding witch and the second was so afraid he might hurt her that she served herself up like a sacrifice.

Sorin tugged on his clothes, knotting the laces in his haste to be away from the Black Tower, from Battlewar Castle. He couldn't run away, the last shreds of his tattered pride wouldn't let him. Without cause, he couldn't go. Not yet.

"By all the fires of the afterlife, by the will of the gods, please bring Staria a great battle. Call me away from this place. I beg of you."

6

Perhaps all his years at the sword did not go completely unnoticed by the eyes of the gods. Sorin jarred against the back of his horse, feeling the pounding beat of the large animal's hooves carrying him away from Battlewar's outer wall. The familiar creak sounded behind him as sentinels lowered the large wood-and-iron gate. The heavy weight of it made for a slow decent, but in time of attack, if the rope were cut as a man rode under, it would impale him and his horse under the deadly weight of the reinforced metal crossbars. Everything about Battlewar Castle had been designed for war, just like everything else in their land—from the long battlements that stretched around the main castle and

Battlewar Town to the secret passages and underground escape routes.

Lady Jayne had disappeared from the castle and, after an extensive search of the grounds, it was decided two small groups of knights would ride after the escaped woman. The others headed north to search for a trail, though it seemed unlikely she'd choose that treacherous route. Already word spread through the town in the outer bailey, and all the residents of Battlewar Town would be on the lookout if she hid within the city walls. Lucky for them, she did not know of the tunnels leading from the castle to outside the walls or how to reach them. It made their search easier. Ronen barely spoke as they looked, but to utter quietly, "My wife has run away. The gods truly frown upon me."

The full moon shone bright over the prairie grasses, giving the knights enough to see by as they rode hard over the fields. Sorin felt sorry for his brother, but couldn't help the selfish relief that he had an excuse to run away from his own torment. As the head of his family, capturing Lady Jayne demanded his attention. He had to go. They would find the woman, Sorin had no doubts about that. Many of the knights trained at Battlewar in their youth, and this prairie and the surrounding forests were extensions of that very education.

The wind hit hard upon his face, whipping Sorin's hair back. Once they crossed the prairie they would spread out into the forest, searching for a sign of her passing. She couldn't have gone far on foot, and most likely her screams would alert the men to her whereabouts. No matter how much or how little Divinity told them, these otherworlders didn't know this land or the dangers that waited in the forest at night.

Ronen rode beside him. Sorin lifted his hand. The trees were near and the ground more treacherous. The small contingency of knights slowed. Pointing first to the east and then to the west, he soundlessly ordered the men to spread out and begin their search. When they were alone, Ronen said, "She does not know what she faces, even with my knife to arm her."

"The forest at night can be a daunting thing," Sorin comforted. "Rest assured in that we are far away from the battlefront. The Caniba tribes will not have ventured this far. One look at a wild beast and she'll scream for us to save her."

"Let's ride," Ronen urged, nudging his horse toward the trees. He pulled his sword from his side, gripping it tight. Sorin followed, veering to the right as they spread out. Each man would remain within whistling distance should the lady be found.

"Keep the lady safe," Sorin whispered to the trees, "but don't let us find her too close to the castle. Let her lead us far away from here."

"He left me?" Lilith frowned, knowing she had no right or reason to be shocked at Sera's grumpy news. The servant glared at her, only taking her hateful eyes off Lilith long enough to glance at the dislodged furniture barrier and trail of trinkets that had fallen off the top when Lilith moved it to the door.

"You're surprised, my lady?" Sera demanded. "Did you expect him to stay when you bar him from your chambers like some kind of—?"

"Of what?" Lilith snapped. Late morning shone through the slit window, lighting the room in a soft-ened glow. The night had been long and dark, as Lilith hovered beneath the covers. Several times she'd dozed, but never for long. Lack of rest made her waspish, and Sera's accusing tone only added to her ill temper. "Like some kind of sane person? You might like to sleep with complete strangers because they picked you out of the lineup, but I actually prefer to know the person. Maybe go out on a date. Have a conversation beyond, 'Take up your skirts for I will do you now'."

Sera gasped, her mouth hanging open. She sputtered before finally managing, "You would question the will of the gods?"

"Sorin is not a god," Lilith assured the woman, jerking at the long sleeve of the black tunic. It unrolled in the night and now hampered her fingers. "Trust me. Everywhere I go, there is some man claiming to be a god."

"No, Lord Sorin is a man of flesh and blood, but the gods choose you for him. You are his reward for great service in battle." Sera searched her face, as if she were a fool not to know about their gods and customs. "Men have needs, especially Starian men. They need passion for it keeps them strong in horrific times. Women are the vessel for release, a means to have children. That is our role. That is our duty. In return, we are protected and provided for."

"What of love?" Lilith asked, almost feeling sorry for the woman. She ran her fingers along the back of the cushioned chair. The small, fine stitching had been done by hand.

"What of it?" Sera waved her hand in dismissal

of the idea. "Should you come to care deeply for him that is up to you, but I would not encourage such affections. It makes losing them in battle harder. Do not expect tenderness or dwell on romantic emotions. It is not in their nature. It goes against everything they've been taught. They will care for you in their way and it is enough."

Enough? A life of mutual convenience was enough for these people? No love?

*How tragic.*

"You are lucky for your husband's station will provide better than others. You do not have to work. It's not so unreasonable a trade." Sera's first irritation lessened, though now she sounded a little annoyed.

"Husband?" Lilith weakened and she barely managed to fall into the chair. "Did you just say he's my... No, that can't be right. No one said anything about getting married. I sure as sunshine would have remembered hearing about that little gem. They said lover and I believe mate was used, but... No."

"Husband, breeding partner, mate, lover, master..." Sera picked up a few of the fallen boxes and bottles and piled them on the bed before going to push at the vanity. Between shoves, she added, "Call it what you will, it all amounts to the same thing. The ceremony is done and you belong to him. He chose you."

The woman had to be wrong. Maybe Sera didn't understand what she was talking about, or perhaps the word "husband" had a different meaning on this dimension. Lilith had run into such confusions before. Language tended to be the same, but it never evolved exactly on each plane. In some cases, a single word could take on a whole new social connotation. Maybe when they said "husband", they meant "man you were partnered up with until he got tired of you and decided to get rid of you".

"I don't belong here," Lilith said, more to herself.

"I don't understand you otherworlders," Sera grumbled. "You get the best of our men and then you complain. If you ask me, you don't deserve them."

*I didn't ask you.*

"Well, if you don't wish to be Lady Lilith, mate of the honorable Lord Sorin, then you can just fend for yourself like any other unattached female. Meals are served below stairs in the main hall. I'll not be carrying up your trays. If you wish for a bath, draw it yourself. And as far as the gowns go, I was going to help you direct the seamstress today, but you can just do that, too." Sera gave the vanity one last push, setting it into place. Then, huffing, she stomped from the room and didn't look back.

"They're all crazy," Lilith whispered, standing to grab the items off the bed. She placed them on the vanity, randomly organizing them. "And they're going to make me crazy, too."

LILITH CAME to believe that Sera only gave idle threats. Sure, the servant never carried a tray back up to the Black Tower, but another maid did. The dry bread and cold meats was hardly a feast, but Lilith fashioned them into a decent enough sandwich. However, that had been hours ago and the pains of hunger were slowly creeping in. What she wouldn't do for a large fettuccine Alexus with crusted bread and garlic. Just thinking about it made her mouth water.

Soon after Sera's huffy departure, the seamstress, Fantine of Battlewar, arrived with an entourage of workers in tow. She'd been horrified to see the black tunic Lilith wore for a dress and instantly demanded the lady remove it. Lilith refused until another gown could be brought in to replace it, even then demanding they give her privacy. The people of

Staria might like to walk around naked, but Lilith lived in San LoFrancis, and there people wore clothes. Lots of them.

Fantine worked with a mind of her own, asking questions but then deciding her own answers. She spoke in rapid half-sentences that her helpers appeared to translate, but that left Lilith with a slight headache.

"I told you, I'm not wearing a low neckline," Lilith tugged at the soft tan material of the tunic dress she tried on. The garments were readymade, just in need of a few alterations. Lilith placed her hand on her chest. "I want it to cover here."

"That is not the fashion." Fantine shook her head in disapproval, pointing at a dark blue corset. A soft-spoken brunette with short curls handed it to her. "What pleasure is that to...?" The words trailed off.

Precise, nimble fingers clipped material deftly into place as the seamstress fitted material around Lilith's slightly protesting body. She pulled the corset tight, constricting Lilith's waist and making her gasp.

"Eyes," one of the helpers said as she studied the outfit.

"Agreed." Fantine nodded. "More blues."

"Blues," the others repeated in unison.

"More here." Lilith again patted her bare chest.

The corset thrust her breasts up, like it did on the other women. Glancing around, she grabbed a wide scrap of material off the bed and wrapped it around her shoulders before tucking the two ends into the front bodice to create the affect of a shirt. "See."

All the women tilted their heads to the side at once. Fantine frowned. The others bit their lips.

"We got what we require," the seamstress announced, waving her hand for the others to follow. They scurried to pick up their messes before rushing out the door.

Now that she was alone, she studied the quiet chamber. Lilith normally adapted to new surroundings and sounds. She had to with her job. This place was different. The silence pressed in on her, broken only by the occasional whisper of the wind against the window slits. The fireplace in both her and Sorin's room were barren, causing a chill to settle in the tower.

Dressed modestly in her new gown, shawl, and blue corset, Lilith found herself in Sorin's chamber. She thought it sad that so much of his life focused on war—from the beliefs of his people to the arsenal of blades attached to his wall. Where were the photographs? Or the paintings of loved ones and ancestors? Where were the books or games? Did the man do anything outside of battle? Nothing in the room told her about the man she now lived with. Did he have hobbies? Aspirations? Or perhaps the lack of personal belongings was more telling than not. Maybe a knight didn't have aspirations for the future because they didn't believe they would have a future.

When she carefully dug through his trunk, desperate for a hint of the man who lived there, she found a neat stack of clothing atop a folded blanket. Armor and chainmail dominated most of the space, some shiny with elaborate carvings and others tarnished and worn by time. A few of the chest plates had puncture holes in them.

Thinking about it made Lilith's head spin. She became desperate to discover something, *anything*, about Sorin's human side. So far, all she'd seen was a dominating warrior with questionable restraint when it came to sex.

"I don't belong here." Lilith closed the lid, leaving everything the way she'd found it. She wrapped her arms around her stomach. The idea of forever in Staria scared the hell out of her. She hadn't been bred for this life. Giving in to weakness, she leaned her head down and began to cry. "Please, Divinity, get me out of here. I didn't screw up this bad. I don't deserve this. I don't belong here."

Four days. Four very long, emotional days. And she spent them completely and utterly alone.

Lilith stared at her fingers, refusing to look around the main hall. She missed Jayne and Karre, even Paige. At any rate, she missed the idea of them. They would have understood her position, the stranger set on display before a group of very moody, very accusing knights and their women.

For the most part, no one talked to her. After the seamstress's visit, she hadn't had anywhere near a real conversation. The few who ventured the occasional words did so with disdain, some with open hostility. They made her feel like evil incarnate, and all because she wouldn't fuck their most beloved warrior.

They allowed her full access to the castle and she spent hours during the day exploring, analyzing her situation and searching for a way home. She even pressed against the walls, looking for secret rooms like her bathroom. She found none. Her natural curiosity made her perfect for her job. Torches, fireplaces and narrow windows remained the main sources of light wherever she went. She could only imagine that the Starians had spent so much time on perfecting war that they spent little effort on other technologies.

Inside the castle, a large kitchen buzzed with constant activity. If they weren't serving one of the two main meals of the day, the cooks stayed busy baking breads and pastries. Lilith loved the smell outside the kitchen and would have taken a closer look had her presence warranted more of a welcome. Accessible from the kitchen, castle gardens and a small fruit orchard spread out over an enclosure.

Below stairs, there were sewing chambers with enormous looms and sewing tables, a laundry room with a boiling pit of the dark blue water, quarters for servants, and walk-in linen closets. The shelves were filled with sheets carefully labeled with various coat-of-arms and symbols. Larders and dry storage overflowed with food and drink. Should there be a siege, Battlewar would definitely stand independent for many months.

Stairs led down to a dark dungeon, one she could only see through the barred window on the thick door. When she tried to get a better look, Brock chased her away. The accommodations were much worse than her initial holding cell.

Several private towers, like the one she lived in, lifted high over the castle. Then, directly above the hall, smaller apartments were set for the knights of lesser rank and their families. Her welcome there had been just as cold, as she walked the long hallway and peeked inquisitively inside any open doors.

One mother had even gone so far as to shield her smiling little boy, warning, "Stay away from the witch or she'll curse your sword hand." The cute smile faded to be replaced by instant fear.

*Harlot or witch.* Lilith gave a sardonic laugh. *Great options.*

If the days were bad, the nights were horrific. Lilith lay those long hours, alone in her tower, surrounded by darkness and plagued by her own mind. It became impossible not to think of Sorin, of how she was expected to give herself to him. Then she'd remember his kisses, passionate, demanding and completely overwhelming.

There, in the relative safety of her bed, surrounded by the dancing firelight and shadows, she allowed herself to fantasize. She hadn't seen him naked, not even bare-chested, but her imagination could fill in what she didn't know. Many of the men had tattoos on their arms and flesh littered with scars.

"Sorin," she'd whisper, feeling foolish now that she thought about it in daylight. In her fantasy, he made love to her slowly, tenderly. His thick, strong body would stretch out on top of hers, their legs entwined. Hands ventured over every inch of flesh, tracing muscles and discovering secrets.

Lilith adjusted her hips, pressing her legs tightly together as she adjusted her skirt. A few of the knights stared at her as she reached for a drink. The maids thought it odd she insisted on juice for the evening meal instead of liquor. As appealing as drunken oblivion sounded, the last thing Lilith needed was to be inebriated.

Her mind wandered once more as she set the goblet down. Sorin's restraint surprised her and the more she thought about it, the more impressed she became. The feel of his cock, pressing at the entrance of her pussy as they lay in the stairwell, haunted her. There were so many other ways she could have handled that situation.

In reality, she doubted she'd ever fuck a man in the stairwell of a castle, but in her fantasies the idea was arousing. She closed her eyes and leaned her head against the high back of the chair. Part of her wished he would have just thrust and taken her, not giving her a choice but to let him ride her. She shivered, forcing the thought from her mind, sure she'd prefer the soft and gentle version of her dreams.

Battlewar loomed like a dark omen over Lord Sorin's head. His brother stayed behind with a few of the others, not ready to come back as he rode to tell the king about the Caniba spies they encountered in the forest. Seeing the blood staining his hand, Sorin wished he could have been the one to ride for the southern borders.

Seated upon his steed, Sorin waited in hopes that Ronen would send for him. The harsh lines of the castle stood firm against the streaked magenta-orange sky. The three knights who traveled back to the castle with him were already well into the outer bailey, and the sentinels guarding the wall stared at him in curiosity, holding the gate open.

Sorin didn't want to ride in. Lilith was in there, in his home, invading his life. His cock pulsed, never satisfied, always half erect, but he determined he couldn't touch her, no matter how much he wanted to. If he dared, he'd not be able to stop. Even in his dreams, he had no control with her. Each night when he closed his eyes, he'd picture himself behind her, thrusting like a madman, pounding violently into her until he came, only to do it again and again.

*Why have the gods cursed me?*

A sentinel lifted his arm, gesturing toward the open gate. Sorin blinked, needlessly looking back in hopes of an escape. No rider came for him, and he found himself nudging the horse forward before turning back around to face his fate. Ignoring the quizzical expressions of the guards, he kept his back straight and his eyes forward. He had to look a fright, covered in dirt and blood, but it wasn't anything the people of Battlewar Town hadn't seen before.

Through the corner of his eyes, he saw people in the town pointing at him from outside their closely set homes. Intermingled with the homes in the outer bailey were a couple of barns, many workshops, small breweries and a large marketplace where the commoners sold their wares. A few of the soldiers lifted their hands in greeting.

Sorin slowed his horse as a little girl ran after a chicken. Her pretty dress was covered in mud and she gave him an impish smile. All he could manage was a nod in return. Her smile fell somewhat. As one of the few female children, she'd be used to more attention.

"Curse the witch, my lord!" a peasant woman yelled, pointing her finger in the air. Dark, small eyes watched him from within a sea of hard wrinkles.

"We'll sacrifice a goat to send her back to the otherworld!"

"Yea, my lord!" an old man next to her added, just as drunkenly. "Curse the witches that bring unhappiness to your home!"

Sorin's brow furrowed in surprise. It would seem rumors had spread while he was gone.

"Bless Lord Sorin! Bless Lord Ronen!" another voice added, calling over the distance. He couldn't see who screamed it. "Curse the witches!"

A round of agreement seemed to move over the street, traveling away from him throughout the town. "Curse the witches! Curse the witches!"

"Bless you as well," Sorin answered, hoping to quiet some of the whispers with words of his own. The king would not be pleased to hear the people of his most beloved city had revolted against the two brides of Firewall. "But they are merely foreign wives, not witches. They will learn our ways."

*One can only pray.*

"Wives are witches, my lord," the old man cackled. "You just haven't been married long enough to see it!"

"Eh!" the woman next to him screamed in protest, instantly throwing a tankard of ale at his head. "I have four men waiting in line to replace you. We're all just waiting for you to drop."

The man ducked and began to run down the muddy street. "See what I mean!"

Beyond the market, in the center of the city, a second, shorter wall encircled the inner bailey yard and castle. Contained within were the exercise yard where the knights trained, a small chapel, and the stables. Sorin found himself riding abnormally slow as he passed through the inner gate. Young pages ran for him, eager to take his reins so that he may dismount and go inside. Their eyes lit with boyish excitement to see the blood-stained tunic their lord wore.

The towheaded page nudged the darker one, prompting him to ask, "Did you slaughter Ronen's witch, my lord?"

*By all the bloody battleaxes in Staria.*

Sorin sighed heavily, swinging his leg over the back of the horse and tossing over his reins. "I did not see any witches, but my sword did meet Caniba spies."

The boys nodded in excitement, whispering fervently as they hurried to take care of his horse. He desperately wanted a drink, but didn't dare enter the main hall to face more curses or worse—his wife.

Slipping around the side of the castle, he ducked under a narrow entryway mostly used by maids carrying wet laundry outside to dry.

"My lord," a servant gasped in surprise to see him. She gave a small curtsey. "Is there aught I can do for you?"

"Here." He pulled his tunic over his head, glad to be rid of it. Tossing it at her, he asked, "Where is Lady Lilith?"

"In the main hall for the evening meal, I believe, my lord," the woman answered. "Would you like me to fetch her?"

"No. Leave her. Have someone bring food to the Black Tower."

"And your bath?" she asked.

"I'll use the one in my lady's room," he answered, not wanting to wait for someone to cart up his usual metal tub.

## 7

"Lord Sorin beheaded four Caniba spies in the forest with no help from the others. Sir Traven said he is possessed and the men who rode with him are in a dark mood because of it. Sir Traven said they should have taken at least one of the Caniba men alive so they might discover what they were doing this far north. It's true what they say, that witch Lady Lilith cursed him into madness."

"Those in town say we should dunk her in the river. If she comes to the surface, she's a witch. It's the only way to be rid of that kind."

"Not true. There's always fire. Witches burn faster than humans."

"And the other? Lady Jayne? Did they find her?"

"Dead, too, for all I know. And good riddance for the poor Lord Ronen."

Lilith didn't know the maids who spoke, as she waited on the tower stairwell, just out of eyesight but close enough to eavesdrop on their conversation. She strained to hear more, but they walked off. A sick feeling curled in her stomach. Sorin decapitated four men in a fight and they blamed her for it?

"I don't belong here. I don't belong here," she repeated, whispering the mantra as if saying the words could make the land of Staria disappear.

Her legs ached, the muscles still adjusting to the endless progression of steps. By the time she made it to the top, she longed for nothing more than the warmth of her bed and the secret fantasies of her late night dreams, tucked away from the spiteful eyes of the hall.

The soft glow of firelight shone from her room. It wasn't unusual as someone usually lit it at night. For all its barbaric tendencies, Battlewar Castle flowed to a unique rhythm perfected by time and practice. Things were done, even when you didn't see someone doing them.

"I don't belong here," she said under her breath as she entered her room.

Lilith tugged at the scarf around her neck.

Fantine had matching ones made for all her new gowns, though some were so fine and thin their transparency did little to provide cover. The material trailed behind her as she absently dropped it on the end of the bed and walked across the room to the window. She peered out the slit, seeing a few trees and plenty of darkening sky. Stars poked in from the heavens, just starting to shine through.

"Why did you send me here?" Lilith moaned. She'd worked so hard for the company, had done her job, gathered information and they were going to punish her like this for one, little, stupid accident? Feeling helpless, she hit her hand on the stone wall, slapping it. "I don't belong with these people."

"Is my lady too high for us?"

*No.* Lilith stiffened. *It can't be.*

Almost afraid to look, she slowly turned to face the room. Her eyes went to the doorway. He wasn't there. Her heart quickened and she fought to control the breathiness in her tone. "Lord Sorin?"

He didn't answer, but movement caught her attention and she turned to the tub. Sorin sat in the dark blue of the water, his arms stretched to the side. His wet hair slicked back from his face, revealing the stark lines of his features. She bit her lip and pressed her legs tightly together. Firelight danced over his flesh, molding to each and every dip and curve. A black tattoo wound his upper arm, the lines bold and confident just like the man.

Lilith shivered. She hadn't fantasized about him in there, but it was possible he wasn't real. Right?

"Leave me," Sorin closed his eyes and leaned his head back.

Wrong.

Lilith tried to make her legs move, but they kept her rooted to the floor. Curiosity urged her forward, to try to see beneath the water's surface. The brawny muscles of his chest and neck called to her hands. In her current situation it had been hard not to think of his naked body over hers. Those images came back to her now and a deep longing filled her. She parted her lips, almost feeling the wet glide of flesh against them as she imagined kissing his neck.

*He's a stranger*, her logical mind argued.

*He doesn't feel like a stranger*, her treacherous body replied.

Lilith tried to think of something to say to break the silence and slow her departure. "I'm not a witch."

His head lifted and he arched a brow.

"Apparently the people in town are under the impression I'm a witch and wish to drown or burn me to find out for sure. I can assure you, I'm not a witch." She dared a few steps closer, her eyes glancing down into the water. The darkness kept him from view. Not really paying attention to her words, she continued, "Not that there is anything wrong with witches. I've met some very nice ones on other planes. Then again, I've met some bad ones. Anyway, I'm not one."

He didn't move.

Lilith took another step forward. "So I guess what I'm saying is I'd like to know if you have a library I can look at. A records room? Scroll lock? Database?"

Still nothing. No response beyond the aggravatingly straightforward look.

"I'd like to read over your laws to know what my options are." Lilith was about to go closer when his words stopped her.

"Your option is to let me protect you," he stated. "As your husband, it is my duty."

She flinched. *There's that husband word again.*

"That's kind of you to offer, but I'd still like to read—"

"Please, drop the deceptions. You wish to find a way out of our joining. There is no way out, save death." Again he closed his eyes, looking very weary as he sighed. "Perhaps you will become lucky and I will perish in battle."

"Don't say that," she snapped. Lilith leaned against the opened bathroom wall and it moved under her weight, making her pull instantly back. "I never wished you dead. I have never wanted anyone dead. Well, there was this boy, Billy Holliday, who sat behind me in grammar school and used to flick eraser bits at me, but... Is it true you cut off four guys' heads because of me?"

"Did you send the Caniba spies into the Hanging Forest?"

"No."

"Then it was not because of you," he answered reasonably.

Somehow, without her realizing it, she'd come to stand beside the tub. The bathroom seemed small with both of them in it. Heat radiated from the water, contrasting the cooler air flow from a window. Lilith still hadn't figured out how to open and close the window slits. "Is your bad mood with the men because of me?"

His eyes opened and he surged to his feet. "By the teeth of the damned, woman, I asked you to leave."

Rivulets cascaded down his flesh, creating wet

trails that her eyes delightedly followed. The scars continued from his neck down, attesting to a dangerous life. Firelight caught on the water, decorating his entire length with tiny dots and trails of light. His broad chest tapered to a thick, tight waist, which in turn molded into perfect hips. But it wasn't his hips that made her stop and stare. His cock stood tall and proud, so erect that veins had risen along the sides.

"Do not look at me like I am about to attack you," he growled.

"You're not?" Lilith wondered at the disappointment in her tone.

"Not if you go now. I am aware you do not wish for me in your bed, and I will not go where I'm not wanted." When she didn't move, he stepped over the tub's edge onto the stone step. "But if you think you can escape our dismal fate you are mistaken. The decision has been made. We are joined."

He appeared so forlorn that she couldn't help but reach for him. Her hand slid onto his arm. The muscle flexed.

"I don't mean to insult you, Sorin. It's not you, it's this place. I don't belong here. Normally if I travel to a new dimension it's for work. I go, gather information and then leave. But I was not assigned to come here. I simply went to bed one night and then woke up in your prison." She tried to pull him around to face her, a great feat considering how he towered over her.

"So you are a spy?" he concluded, clearly not pleased by the fact.

"No. I'm a data analyst. I read books and take notes. I analyze facts and create historical profiles of the parallel universe I'm assigned to and then input them into Divinity's central database. When I go to a place, the governments know about it—well, mostly they do. But I assure you, there's no spying involved." Lilith swayed on her feet. His body radiated warmth. The muscle beneath her hand didn't relax. She flexed her fingers, wanting him to look at her. "Why did you choose me? I heard some of the women talking and they said you weren't expected to choose anyone."

"The gods told me to." The words lacked passion, as if they were a simple truth. "If what you say is true about Divinity and they broke their word, we will renegotiate our position with them. As for us, it's too late to change what has happened. Honor forbids it."

Maybe it was the softness of his tone or the romantic cast of firelight against his naked body, but Lilith found herself not caring about freedom quite so much. She slid her hand down his arm to his wrist and leaned her face next to his bicep. He reached around her stomach to her hip, gently pulling her in front of him. Dark eyes bore into her questioningly.

"I'm not very experienced." Heat fanned her cheeks, but she forced her eyes to stay on his. Sorin tightened his grip. His strength radiated up her hip and spread like a spark throughout her body. Moisture gathered in the folds of her sex. "I mean, I know about it, but I haven't, you know, a lot, and you look like you might...uh, hurt."

*By all the weapon thingies they normally curse to, I did not just say that—and to him! How embarrassing. I couldn't sound more like a moron if I tried. Oh please, floor, open up and drop me.*

Lilith wanted to sink into the stone and hide. What was it about him tonight that turned her into a babbling idiot? And why did all her fantasies keep flashing in her mind as laughable examples of what this man was really like during sex?

*I know about it? You look like you might hurt? Oh, Lilith, don't say another thing ever, ever again. Vow of silence from this point on.*

"I mean, you're pretty aggressive." Why was her mouth still moving? And why in the world didn't he just say something to shut her up? Did he just have to stand there, staring at her? "Which I suppose is war training, or at least a side effect of being trained as a warrior. But I'm not a warrior, obviously." She glanced down, suddenly realizing she'd taken the scarf off, and her breasts were thrust together and up by the dark blue of her corset. Torn between acting like she didn't notice and covering up her displayed chest with her hands, she continued, "So I hope you understand what I'm saying."

When she looked up, she found him staring at her chest intently. His lips had parted in quickened breaths. All too aware of his naked body so close to hers and the telltale lift of his towering erection, she tried to take a step back. His hand on her hip tightened, not letting her go.

"Please tell me what you're thinking, Sorin," Lilith whispered. "I can't tell."

He chuckled and lifted a brow. "How incredibly sexy you are in that corset. How much my body aches to be inside of you. How I want nothing more at the moment than to throw you up against the wall and ravish you. How... That's pretty well it."

"Oh," she breathed in mild surprise, not expecting that answer.

He leaned his face toward hers, licking his lips. His hand moved to the small of her back, forcing her next to his taut body. The unmistakable length of his shaft dug into her skirts. He stroked her cheek before pulling her mouth softly to his lips. "Touch me."

Lilith took hold of his arms, using him for support as her legs weakened. The tip of his tongue traced the rim of her mouth, teasing her lips apart with their wet, probing insistence. She savored each movement, each new sensation. A soft moan escaped her. He tasted so good, like sweet wine, and smelled even better.

Sorin cupped her ass, massaging the cheeks firmly so that her thighs pressed forcefully to his. His hips rocked against her skirts. After several moments, he withdrew his lips and brushed them across her cheek to her ear. "Touch me." He took her hand and compelled it between their bodies so that she palmed his arousal. The thick appendage filled her hand. Then, the same guiding hand lifted to her mouth, and he pressed a finger between her moist lips, rubbing them meaningfully several times before hooking her teeth and urging her down. "Finish me."

Lilith's eyes rounded as she got his meaning. He wanted her on her knees so she could suck his cock. Her pussy protested the one-sided idea. Her mouth watered, tempted.

"Finish me, so that I do not lose myself and take

you too hard." He rocked his erection into her hand and groaned. "It is not my wish to hurt."

No man had ever said such a thing to her. The finger slipped from her mouth, wetting her jaw as he reached for the top of her bodice. He grabbed hold, several fingers pushing down between the tight squeeze of her breasts. Her breathing became hard and choppy and her heart beat so hard against her chest, she knew he had to feel it. She waited, wanting his fingers to find their way to her aching nipples. The nubs were erect, puckered and waiting for him.

Lilith found her knees bending under the intensity of his gaze. This had to be a dream, no matter how real he felt. She wasn't like this. She didn't succumb to mindless lust. The erotic placement of his fingers only made her body all the hotter. Each movement stung, sending wave after wave of delicious warmth down to her stomach.

Her fingernails pressed into his sides, raking their way down as she knelt before him. Curse it all, but this man was in perfect shape! He let go of her bodice, reaching to grab his cock and angle it toward her mouth as if he couldn't wait for her to do it herself. He bent his knees to better position himself for pleasure.

Sorin tensed, his stomach tightening in front of

her. Lilith licked the mushroomed tip and he jerked violently, gasping. She flicked her tongue several times to taste the warm, salty essence of him. The power of him flooded her. He was so strong, so virile, such a perfect specimen of masculinity. The feel of the smooth shaft overwhelmed her like a potent sex drug, making her want to take him deeper into her mouth until she choked on the length of him.

Lilith grabbed the extra length of his shaft and moved her lips to meet her fists. Sorin buried his hands in her hair. She sucked, twirling her tongue around the ridge while carefully gauging his response.

Sorin gasped and grunted, communicating his satisfaction in animalistic noises. He arched his back, thrusting into her. The saliva from her mouth wet him as he moved, creating a slick tunnel inside her fists. He worked his body, the full length of him covered in the orange glow of firelight, more so now that the sky outside had darkened.

His hold on her head tightened almost painfully. Lilith sucked harder. Sorin jerked, keeping her mouth locked on his shaft. Crying out, he thrust one last time and released a stream of hot cum into her mouth. He didn't release her, forcing her to swallow the salty essence. When finally he let go, he stumbled back. Lilith licked her lips, the erotic taste of him in her mouth.

"I feel weak," he said in surprise. Lilith's body stung with need, and she didn't feel too strong herself at the moment. She backed toward the bed, sitting the instant the mattress hit the back of her thighs.

Sorin followed her, crawling over her as she fell onto her back. His knees and hands pressed around her, trapping her down. Now that he'd met with release, an almost devious light entered his eyes. A slow, predatory smile curled the side of his mouth. "Where do you think you're going? We are not finished."

Now that he had her, he wasn't letting go. Sorin's body sang with the pleasure of her mouth, but he was only getting started. He sat back, keeping her under him as he tugged at her skirts, pulling them up to free her legs. He settled his knees between her bare thighs to better look at her. The mattress shifted under his weight. After her earlier plea, he promised himself he'd take it slow. His size clearly frightened her. The thought gave him more than a small measure of pride.

The smooth skin of her calves and thighs were unmarked by hardship. He stared openly at her, unashamed and immensely curious. How quickly things seemed to change. When he'd seen her from his place in the tub, he thought her a dream come to torment him. Now the dream had become real, flesh and blood, delicious and sweet.

Lilith brought her upper legs together and pushed her skirts down a few inches. He frowned, not liking the way she hid herself from him. He wanted to look and he intended to do just that.

Sorin again pushed at her skirt, lifting it higher. A narrow strip of shortly cut hair lined her pussy. She had her skirt covering it before he had a chance to really look.

He frowned, persistently endeavoring to uncover his new treasure. Sorin massaged her legs, hoping to relax them open. Breasts strained against her corset, lifting and falling in a mesmerizing rhythm. Everything about her entranced him. She smelled sweet. Her skin was so soft. When she kissed him, she made a small moaning noise that drove him to distraction. He doubted she was even aware that she did it.

Sorin wanted to explore, wanted to see and touch and taste, but she kept hiding herself from him. Lilith angled her hips, moving so the skirt fell back down to hide her pussy. He gave a low growl of frustration.

"You hide," he said, keeping his tone low. Sorin suppressed the animalistic urge to rip at her clothing so she couldn't do it again.

"You're staring," she defended.

Her words made no sense. Of course he stared. He wanted to see. A beautiful woman like her had no reason to hide. Actually, to the men of his country, no woman had a reason to hide.

Coming up with an idea, he grinned and reached for the scarf she'd discarded on the end of the bed. Sorin leaned over her, letting the material slide over her throat. He snaked it over her arm, winding it lightly before moving to the other one. Then, before she realized what he'd done, he pulled both ends and drew her wrists together. Lilith's eyes widened as he quickly bound her arms over her head.

She squirmed beneath him. "What are you doing? Sorin?"

He crawled down her body, stopping when his mouth reached her knee. Blowing against her flesh, he answered, "Kissing you."

"But..." She worked her legs restlessly against the bed.

"I'm taking you prisoner so you can't hide from

me. I wish to look." He grinned, liking the idea of her being under his control. She tried to protest, the weak attempt of someone who didn't believe wholly in the cause they were fighting for. He tore at her gown, ripping the material of the skirt out of his way. The loud noise silenced her as rounded eyes stared at him. The corset held the dress tight to her chest and waist, but exposed the engaging sight of her sex to view.

Sorin took his time, lightly kissing every inch of revealed flesh. He licked along her inner thigh, before settling next to her pussy. Almost shaking with eager excitement, he kissed her sex, letting the taste of her cover his lips. He breathed deeply, intrigued by the very femaleness of her body. Soft, yet toned. Smooth and unscarred. Intoxicatingly sweet.

He licked her hard, moaning into her sex. Lilith arched, gasping as her legs tightened around his head. She pulled at her wrists, trying to break free. Experimenting with this tongue, he twirled it within her slick folds, testing her responses. But soon his tongue wasn't enough. He wanted to touch, too. He slipped a finger inside her, wiggling it as the tight hold of her body gripped him.

Sorin's cock strained, swollen with need, and he

wondered if he'd ever get enough of her. She bucked against his mouth, trembling with release. Cream dripped from her sex, wetting him with her desire. He moaned, crawling up her body, pausing to kiss the tops of her breasts. She squirmed beneath him, her head rolling on the mattress as she blinked lazily in his direction.

Wondrous sensations filled him, ones he didn't care to look too deeply at. He needed to be inside her, to end the torment he'd felt since first feeling her in the hall. Sorin was not a man used to being controlled, but when she looked at him, her lips parted and her cheeks flushed, he felt himself desperate to please her, no matter what she would command of him.

Sorin's thighs forced hers apart. A light sheen of sweat covered their bodies. Lilith tensed as he drew his cock along her slickened folds.

*Easy. Slow. Do not frighten her or she will banish you from her bed.*

With more self-control than he'd ever thought possible, he slipped his hard cock along her yielding sex. Moist heat welcomed him and he gulped. Sorin brushed his mouth to hers, liking the way their tastes mingled in the kiss. He rocked his hips forward, entering her.

*Tight. Hot. Blessed night!*

*Go. Slow.*

Gradually, he eased into her, stretching the tight muscles to fit his girth. Bracing his elbows, he kept his body close, enjoying the contrast of the harder corset to softer flesh against his chest. Lilith accepted his easy pace, her legs relaxing along his waist to let him go deeper. Oh, but it was hard not to just pound into her, taking her rough and fast. Every primal urge inside him told him to ride her, to make her feel every inch, to let her know she'd been claimed.

*Slow. By all the stars in the sky, Sorin, go slow.*

He held his breath. He'd never known a woman to be so tight. Unable to take the torment, his hips flexed on their own accord, seating his cock to the hilt. She gasped and arched, her muscles gripping him.

Sorin worked his hips in shallow thrusts, panting for air as he slid in the wet heat of her pussy. He pushed up for leverage, watching her glorious body beneath his. Her breasts bobbed, and he wished he had a knife to cut them loose from the binding top.

When she didn't protest, he thrust harder. Her body met his. Soft moans of pleasure escaped her. Then, suddenly, she tensed, her entire body going rigid as she met her release. The tremors were too much. Sorin grunted, a loud, primitive noise of power and completion. With a jerk, he emptied himself into her before collapsing forward. He kept his weight on his elbow so as not to crush her.

After his heart slowed and he caught his breath, he reached to untie her hands. She made soft noises, her eyes closed as she cuddled into the bed. Sorin studied her for a moment, knowing if she demanded it he could rise again. But, when her eyes opened, they appeared tired and it was late in the evening. For the time being, his body would have to be sated.

Leaning over, he kissed her once and said, "Good eve, my lady." Rolling off the bed, he walked to his room to sleep.

LILITH WATCHED Sorin walk away from her. The sexy muscles folded and flexed with each step, seductively revealed by firelight. As if they weighed a ton, she struggled to free her heavy limbs from the scarf. Every bone in her body felt as if it had melted. Her nerves tingled with a fantastic numbness and all he could say was good eve? Good freaking eve?! After what they just did he left her for his own bed?

Too tired to chase after him and unsure she'd

have the courage to confront him if she did, she didn't move from her spot on the bed as she reached to pull the laces of her corset. The restrictive clothing made it hard to breathe. Finally free, she flung the material on the floor. The gown would have to do for nightclothes, even with the torn slit up the skirt, for she wasn't getting out of the bed to find something else.

If she hadn't been one hundred percent sure he'd orgasmed, she would have thought she'd done something wrong. In fact, it felt as if they'd done something very, very right. Turning her back on the door, she jerked the covers over her body and snuggled into the mattress, pretending the lump in the folded coverlet was really Sorin resting next to her. Tomorrow she'd analyze what happened. Tonight she just wanted to dream.

## 8

AFTER THEIR EVENING together and his abrupt departure from her bed, Lilith wasn't sure what to expect. Surprisingly, she slept better than she had since she woke up that first morning in Staria. She half expected to be sore after sex, but aside from a mild ache, she felt great.

Nevertheless, with the morning light came her overactive brain's logical demands. What did sex with Sorin mean? Would she be treated differently now by those in the castle? Would they stop calling her a witch? Would Sorin expect her to lift her skirts whenever the mood struck him? What if he did? What if he didn't? And what in the world did she say to him?

Confusion filled her. She felt connected to him

now, but knew she couldn't stay. This wasn't her dimension. Sure, she didn't have much of a life in her own parallel, but it was hers. That's where she belonged. And someone at Divinity owed her an explanation.

With her only way out blocked by Sorin's room, Lilith listened for signs of movement and watched the door in hope that he'd walk in. All was silent.

She took her time getting dressed, bathing, then fussing over which of the dozen outfits to put on. Well, a dozen minus one. Her gown from the evening before had been ruined. She finally decided on a soft cream-colored tunic dress with burgundy corset. The cream material had simple embroidery around the edges, not nearly as decorative as she'd seen on similar garments from other planes. As she looked in the polished metal they had in place of a mirror, she contemplated leaving the scarf off. The thought only lasted a second before she crammed a sheer piece of burgundy material down the front of her bodice.

Still, no sounds came from Sorin's room.

Opening the little containers on the vanity, she found one that she'd determined to be kohl eyeliner. She smudged it lightly over her lids, giving them a smoky effect. Then, braiding her hair into two sections, she wound them at the base of her neck and fastened it with a decorative comb.

And still, no sign that Sorin stirred from his sleep.

Maybe if she tiptoed really quietly, she could sneak downstairs. It might be easier to face him if they weren't quite so isolated in their tower. Morning-afters always tended to be a little awkward, especially, she quickly discovered, when the man she'd slept with was the incredibly confident Lord Sorin.

Slowly pushing open the door, she peeked through the crack. The messy comforter at the end of his bed didn't move. She watched the folds carefully, leaning down to crawl across the floor. Keeping her eyes on the edge of the bed, she inched her way along the stone. When she reached the end, she couldn't stop herself from pushing onto her knees to see if he slept naked. The bed was empty.

Lilith gave a small laugh and stood from the floor. She'd been up since dawn so either he left really early or the insulation between their two rooms was better than she imagined. Recalling how he'd pleasured himself the first day they met, she knew the latter was exceedingly possible.

On her way down, the sounds of footsteps greeted her. Sera appeared, smiling as she balanced a giant tray of food on her shoulder. She again wore a corset that seemed two sizes too small for her generous chest. Steaming miniature bread loafs, red liquid sauce for dipping, sliced meats, fruits, a large bowl of green gelatinous substance, and the biggest flaky pastry she'd ever seen filled the serving tray to capacity.

"Lord Sorin is not in the tower," Lilith said, knowing all that food couldn't be hers. At most, they'd given her dry bread and cold meat trays when she was alone in her room.

"My lord ate below stairs with the men before going out to the exercise field to do mock battle with the squires," Sera explained. "Maray made this especially for my lady to break her fast."

"Really?" Lilith arched a brown in dubious surprise. Why was the woman being so nice to her? "What is it? Poison?"

Sera's smile didn't falter. The servant turned and began the long trek down. "Since you're coming down, I'll bring your tray to the hall. Most of the castle is finished with the morn meal, but I am sure someone will linger for conversation."

"Is there a particular reason you're...?" Lilith stopped. If Sorin went to the hall and announced that he'd gotten a piece of ass from her, she really didn't want to hear it from a gloating, I-told-you-to-listen-to-me Sera. Then again, Lilith had never been completely sure about this maidservant's sanity. "Never mind. Thank you, Sera, and I don't need conversation."

*Like I really want to start my day by being called a witch as people shield their children from me. I have enough to think about without a posse trying to drag me into the courtyard.*

Sera led the way into the main hall. Loud bouts of laughter, not unlike the day Sorin chose her, sounded from within. Lilith approached cautiously, half expecting another group of unwitting females waiting before the crowd. A pang of jealousy hit her as she imagined Sorin choosing another to take her place.

"My lady," a servant greeted, smiling brightly. She carried an empty pitcher in her hands. "Good morn."

"Good..." Lilith didn't finish the thought. What was going on here?

"Good morn, my lady," another woman said, coming from the kitchen with a full tray of food.

"My lady," still a third greeted, nodding her head.

*Welcome to Crazyville, please be sure to wear your padded suit.*

When the fourth maid tried to hurry past with the same happy greeting, Lilith grabbed her arm to stop her. "I'm not being burned alive today, am I?"

"My lady?" the young woman inquired, perplexed. Her brown eyes reminded Lilith of a fuzzy baby animal begging to be picked up. Lilith had noticed the maid before, hanging back from the others when the hall became too boisterous.

"The villagers wanted to burn me as a witch," Lilith explained. "That's not happening today, is it?"

"Oh, you knew about...?" The maid cleared her throat. "No one really thought you were a witch, my lady. I do not think we would have burned you. Lord Sorin made it clear this morning you were not to be touched."

"He made an announcement?" She gave a weak, disbelieving laugh. Well, he did promise to protect her.

"Yea, my lady, he decreed that he inspected you quite thoroughly and you were most assuredly not a witch, and there was to be no drowning or burning of his wife." Her grin widened knowingly. "We all thank you for taking the fire out of his temper."

Lilith made a weak noise by way of an answer,

unsure whatever she said was a coherent series of words. Sorin made an announcement? Sure, she assumed people might suspect something, eventually, but she didn't expect a formal decree of her bedding.

Hurrying inside, she kept her head down in hopes that she wouldn't be noticed making her way to the head table. She always hated being the center of attention, set high above the others as if on display. The crowd was abnormally large for so late in the morning. At her glances, several of the women stood to wave at her. Many of them wore scarves draped over their necks, just as Lilith had been doing.

"My lady!" a loud knight called, lifting his goblet toward her. She flinched as the loud sound turned every pair of eyes to her. She lifted her hand, giving a halfhearted wave of acknowledgement. She scanned the hall for Sorin, relieved when she didn't see him.

Lilith sat at the table in front of the food Sera laid out for her, all too aware of being the center of attention. She'd seen societies, especially ones where people lived in such close proximity, where everyday happenings of the individual were common knowledge throughout the population. But she'd always watched from the edge of their social circles, taking her notes. Now it would seem she was one of the top celebrities. If the negative attention made her uncomfortable before, constant stares and waves made her want to jump up and scream.

Her hand shook as she reached for the bread. The crowd stared openly at her, taking in her every move with wide smiles and avid attention. She much preferred the moody accusations as they refused to acknowledge her. Tearing off a bit of the crust, she stuck the dry morsel in her mouth. The staring didn't stop.

*Is this some kind of new torture? Attention me to death?*

A group of women stood from one of the front tables and slowly made their way forward. The same group had gone out of their way to snub her in the halls a few days before. Whispering and giggling, they pushed a tall, thin blonde to the front. Greta curtsied, saying meekly, "My lady."

Lilith didn't move as she fingered her bread. Greta looked to her companions. They shook their heads and motioned her to speak.

Greta cleared her throat. "We wish an audience."

Lilith looked behind them to the full hall and stated dryly, "You have one."

Greta relaxed. "It is our wish to welcome you properly to Battlewar."

"All right," Lilith began. "Thank—"

"With a fire celebration," Alana asserted, jumping a little in excitement.

Lilith didn't move, as she thought dryly, *They want to set me on fire. I knew it.*

"May we?" Karima asked when Lilith didn't answer.

Refusing to agree to anything she didn't know about, she shook her head in denial. "No."

As if they were all struck by the same magical gale, their expressions fell. Losing all gaiety as they slumped back to their table, the women rejoined their men. Alana went so far as to pull the scarf from her neck and throw it down in an open display of pouting.

Feeling somewhat vindicated for the snubbing, Lilith tore off another piece of bread and dipped it into the red sauce. Maybe this celebrity thing wouldn't be too bad.

BEING a celebrity blew like the geysers on dimensional plane 237.

The small fire celebration victory lasted all of two minutes before the staring and waving resumed. Lilith could barely force herself to swallow, feeling like they counted every bite. By the time a loud ruckus came from the back of the hall, she was ready to kiss the feet of whoever took the attention from her.

Sorin.

The name caught on her lips. Towering over a group of shirtless men, he strode boldly into the main hall, dominating everything around him. In the light of day he appeared handsomer than before—his sweat-glistened chest, the tight fit of his breeches, the thick line of his tattooed arm.

Wet heat pooled between her thighs. Her pussy was all too ready to remind her of the night before. Thick, tight muscles. Strong, sure hands. Firm, smooth ass. Hard, delicious cock. Being tied at his mercy as he ripped her clothing.

Unlike other times, he actually smiled. The expression lit up his entire face, gentling the harsh, disapproving lines. She struggled for breath, drawing in raspy gasps of air through her parted lips. This couldn't be the same man who randomly chose her from a line of women. He appeared too...happy.

The knights made slow progression, filtering through the crowd, stopping to talk and laugh. A warrior with a missing hand spoke to Sorin, pointing his wrist toward the front of the hall. Sorin's smile dropped some as he looked at her over the crowd only to resume the second his gaze met hers. Heat flooded her features.

Sorin strode through the hall, heading in a straight line to where she waited. She bit her lip, trying to think of something clever to say and all too aware of their audience. He came around the table, practically leaping up the platform steps. Dipping his finger into the green substance she had yet to touch, he brought it to his mouth and sucked lightly.

"Good morn, my lady," he said quietly, leaning to kiss her. His eyes glowed with an inner light, drawing her toward him.

Lilith almost let him, but her eyes drifted over the watchful eyes. On instinct, she jerked away, denying him. A low murmur started over the crowd. Sorin stiffened, hurt flitting across his expression before his mouth dropped into the impassable mask she was used to seeing.

"I understand." The flat statement landed on her like a death sentence, hard and condemning. All around the main hall, smiles faded into irritated frowns, as if the whole lot of Starians were joined emotionally to Sorin's moods.

"Sorin, I—" Lilith peered over the watchful faces. "We need to talk."

He crossed his arms over his chest and arched a brow. The motion yanked her gaze down to his thick, tan chest. She flexed her fingers, aching to touch him.

"Not here," she answered, standing. Her feet couldn't carry her fast enough.

Once out of the hall, she started to go to the stairs only to turn around, start for the kitchen, stop and finally decide on the hall she'd last seen Jayne disappear down. She paced nervously, feeling Sorin before he rounded the corner. The man had an energy about him.

Her stomach fluttered. Perhaps alone wasn't such a great idea. Crossing his arms over that mammoth chest, he said nothing. She went to him, closing the distance. Heat wrapped round her, like a million tiny fingers pulling her into him.

"This isn't going to work for me." Lilith moaned softly. That didn't exactly come out right. "I mean to say, we should discuss—"

"I do not see what there is to discuss. You changed your mind about us." His features were as hard as ice and his eyes just as cold. The man was like a broken faucet, hot and cold, cold and hot.

"That's just it," Lilith exclaimed. "This whole 'us' idea. We just met, Sorin."

"The gods willed—"

"No." She held up her hand. It pressed against the hard flank of muscle over his heart. The steady beat drummed against her fingers, contrasting the erratic rhythm in her own chest. "Not the gods, not the knights or their women, you. I don't know you."

"You knew me well enough last night." Was she mistaken or did some of the sparkle come back to his gaze at that statement? He reached for her hip, jerking her against him. Her hand crushed between their bodies. With a swift turn, he had her pinned to the wall. "Should I remind you?"

"That's different. That's..." Lilith struggled to define what last night was. She pushed at his chest, but wasn't able to push him away. His heartbeat quickened as the length of his cock grew thick against her stomach. "It was sex."

"Good sex," he offered, rocking into her.

"Ah, fine." Lilith suppressed a moan. Did he not realize someone could walk around the corner and see them? Starians really had no sense of modesty. None. "However, that's not the issue."

"So you admit that it was good between us." The side of his mouth curled in self-satisfaction. He licked his mouth, his tongue taking a leisurely route along the supple lips.

"I admit that...that is not the issue," she tried to

focus. Why couldn't he just listen to her? Why did he have to look at her with those piercing eyes? Press that gorgeous body still bulging from a workout against her? She swallowed, her mouth suddenly dry. "Sex is sex. Strangers have it all the time, but people are acting like we're a couple."

"We are a couple," he said, his tone aggravatingly certain. "You are my wife."

"Please, Sorin, not here. This is the kind of thing I wanted to talk to you about. I don't want to sit up at the high table. I don't want people watching me all the time."

"You pulled me aside to tell me you don't like your chair?" He chuckled, the sound low and incredibly seductive. "Very well. You will receive a new one."

"It's not the chair. It's the staring and waving and watching and people trying to talk to me and..." She didn't want to move. When he was next to her, she didn't think about freedom or escaping. She couldn't see past his eyes. "Do marriages last forever in Staria?"

To her surprise, he let her go. She stayed against the wall, watching him put distance between them. "You cannot end the marriage."

"This is what I'm talking about. This whole 'us'

issue. You make these definite decrees but you don't tell me why. You don't even answer my questions. I didn't ask how to get out of our arrangement." Calling what they had a marriage seemed strange. "I just asked if marriages, here in Staria, lasted forever."

"Until death." He gritted his teeth. "Women especially are expected to find another mate. So you do not wish to end the marriage?"

It was her turn to refuse to answer outright. "We don't know each other. We skipped a lot of important steps here. I just want to get to know you. Is that such an outlandish request?"

"What 'steps'?" The ice melted by small degrees from his face, and she got the distinct impression that he chuckled inwardly at her. "What is it you want to know?"

"Like, why me? Why did you pick me? Be honest and don't say the gods." She held up a finger in warning. "Unless they walk in the front door and say, 'hey, it's us, the gods, I don't want to hear their opinion in the matter."

He sighed, nodding once. "Very well. I did not plan to take a wife but realized it was time. Duty demands I lead by example and that I have sons to carry on my name and position. Should I die and Ronen as well, there will be none left to lead in our places. The Firewall armies will fall to another, and the hope and sacrifice of our noble ancestors will be forever buried in the past. Staria's defenses could weaken and the Caniba tribes could finally make their way across our borders in full force. Plus, by taking you, I do not have to continue to go to the marriage ceremonies. I can stay on the battlefront with my men."

War. She asked why she was chosen and the answer was war. Lilith bit her lips and looked to the floor. Well, she had wanted honesty. It wasn't exactly a profession of love at first sight.

Sorin leaned over, forcing her to once again meet his gaze. "You are disappointed in my answer. You asked for honesty."

"I know I did. It's not like I expected you to profess love or break into song or anything." She gave a nervous laugh, almost wishing she hadn't asked to learn more. "That would be ridiculous."

"Love?" His arms dropped to his sides, tilting his head in question.

"You don't know what that is?" How sad. "A man and woman meet, over time they have feelings that aren't just physical..."

"I understand the concept. Many of the women brought to us by the fairies speak of romantic love and it is written in our legends. Most marriages even foster genuine affection over time, but our ways do not give consequence to such notions. Marriages are unions. Women need men to protect them, to fight so they do not have to. Men need children and physical release. We stay faithful because the gods demand discipline. War demands discipline."

No wonder the man left her bed with hardly a word. She was pretty much a concubine with privileges of his station. Whatever girlish hope she'd refused to acknowledge died a little. Sorin offered sex, which admittedly was a great checkmark in the plus category. He offered protection so long as he lived. But what if he died? The thought caused tears to well in her eyes. She blinked them back. In this war torn land it was a great possibility that a solider would parish in battle. Then what? She had to go "marry" the next guy who grabbed her arm and said, "mine"? What if the next guy wasn't so restrained? Or smelled funny? Or happened to be a pig farmer who lived forever and condemned her to an eternity of mucking pens?

*I really don't belong here.*

Lilith trembled. She didn't want anyone else to claim her. Out of all the men in this dimension, Sorin definitely ranked as a top catch, if she ignored the fact that he'd never come to love her and she'd been chosen on impulse more than emotion.

"You do not speak." He pulled her attention back to him by slipping a finger under her chin. "Is that all you wished to know?"

Lilith thought about lying, but he'd been honest with her. She could at least return the gesture. "No."

"What else?" He inched closer.

"I'm not sure. Some things can't be learned from a series of questions, Sorin, but from time. Perhaps we could do something together."

His eyes lit with interest. "Something?"

"Not that something, something else." Even as she denied it, the idea had great merit. "Something fun."

"I need to bathe, you may join me." He grinned, unmistakably aroused.

"Like doing something outside, fully clothed."

"A ride?" he offered. "Treacherous Pass should be dry."

"I don't ride," she said.

"You wish to," he thought for a moment before finishing, "practice with blades?"

Lilith shook her head in denial. "I don't blade."

"No blades?" Sorin questioned in disbelief. "Not even a knife? Dagger? Short sword?"

"I'm a fair aim with a gun, but that's it." Shooting had been a required course in her academy training before hiring on with Divinity.

"Gun?"

"Never mind." The last thing Lilith was going to do was add to their arsenal of war implements. They could find their own ways to hurt each other. She frowned. What had Divinity been thinking? Sending her here with all she knew of the other planes. What if she introduced nuclear science or showed them how to make gunpowder? And not just her, but the other women as well. They could really injure a whole society by helping it to advance too quickly.

"What do you think about when you look like that?" His finger slid over her jaw in a light caress. He furrowed his brow and scrunched his nose, mimicking her.

Lilith gave a halfhearted shrug. "I analyze and take mental notes of things. It's how I process...it's not interesting."

"You are female," he declared as if it was a great discovery. "I will take you to Battlewar market. Women like the market."

Lilith smiled at his expectant look and nodded. The man seemed very proud of himself. She envisioned rows of sword blades and battle axes with matching sheathes. They'd probably throw in inducements like free blade sharpeners with every sword purchase. "Sounds perfect."

*Okay, so one lie won't hurt.*

"I must bathe first." Sorin began to back away. "Lady Alana has requested a private audience with you. She is waiting—"

"Audiences, by nature, are public," Lilith broke in, not wanting to talk to the woman.

"It means they wish permission to speak to you. I believe they desire to have a fire ceremony. As the highest-ranking lady in the castle, you must approve."

"Permission?" Lilith frowned. "They didn't need permission to call me a witch and hurl insults. I don't see why I should give them permission to talk."

"That was before we—"

"Don't say it!" Lilith held up her hands. "I'll go audience them and tell them no."

"Fire ceremonies are well received by the townsfolk. It would be a nice gesture, a gift if you will from their new lady." Sorin gave a small bow and hurried from the hall. She detected his feet hitting hard on the stone as he rushed up the tower steps.

How fitting would that be? A fire ceremony for the people who wanted to burn her as a witch.

"My lady?" Lady Alana came around the corner,

as if she'd been waiting for Sorin to leave. Lilith thought it a good thing she didn't give in to the desire to kiss him. It might not have stopped there. Sorin already proved himself to be a man willing to plea-sure her no matter where they were at.

"I'll give you an audience, Lady Alana," Lilith lifted her chin up in the air and brushed past the woman. "Tomorrow."

## 9

THE BRIGHT DAY brought with it a perfect mixture of sunny warmth and cool breeze. Battlewar market teemed with activity. Permanent booths of the local tradesmen clustered together to form narrow walkways impossible to pass through on horse. They butted against the inner bailey wall, packed tight with merchandise. To the south, off the main road through town, traveling merchants set up horse-drawn carts, side by side, and sold wares out of the back. They decorated them with brightly colored strips of material to draw the eye.

A woman with flowers sang loudly, not the songs of Staria but from whatever land the fairies brought her. She paused long enough to lean over to a group of men and receive a kiss from each of them.

"So not everyone is a warrior," Lilith observed from his side. "Inside the castle they made it sound like every man went to war."

Sorin tried to act nonchalant, but it was hard not to reach over and lift Lilith from the ground to twirl her about. She was light enough. He could carry her for miles and never get tired. The breeze caused the scarf around her neck to flutter, lifting just enough for him to get a glimpse of a lifted breast. "Not by daily trade, but most have fought in battle and would answer the call to arms should the king command it."

He escorted her past the booths, enjoying the way she tried not to get excited about a stack of scrolls and giant silver-edged books, yet completely glanced over a stack of lace and ribbons. When she accepted his offer to take her to market, he'd been ecstatic to know she would let him show her as his wife for the whole town to see. And see they did. Wherever Lilith walked people stared and pointed and tried to get her attention with a smile. She acknowledged everyone with a little wave, but didn't seem pleased by it. More often than not, Lilith would try to hide in the shadows or turn his direction down the less crowded path. Being born into his position, Sorin thought nothing of the attention.

At first, it seemed odd that she wanted to "know

him" and he had a difficult time making conversation flow. Bianka had never tried to know him. She just took what she wanted and left him with a tattered reputation. Normally, with the other knights, he would discuss battles, training, wenching, tournaments, duty and honor, or generally cursed the Caniba tribes. Lilith wanted to know about him—what he thought about living in a castle surrounded by so many people, if he liked a particular shade of blue, if he read books or sang or played games or did any number of un-knightly type things. But the more she talked, the more he realized he didn't have much of these other things in his life. Castles were acceptable, but he'd lived most of his life in an encampment inside a tent and surrounded by nature. Blue was a fine enough color, but he preferred the red of his family crest. He read missives from the king, sang drinking songs around a campfire and he played games, but they were tournaments designed to enhance battle skills.

With each answer he gave, he saw a pitying wave cross over her eyes. He didn't like it. Any other woman would be proud of his accomplishments and life. Lilith appeared sad for him, but she never said anything about it beyond a nod of her head and a thoughtful, "Oh."

"Can I ask you something else?" Lilith paused near the end of a cart selling raw leather and touched a couple of pieces.

"Yea." Sorin suppressed a smile. She'd been asking him questions all day. Seeing the merchant, he pointed down to a stack of leather strips, held up two fingers and pointed toward the castle. The man nodded, not moving from his place next to the cart. Like always, Lilith didn't seem to notice his purchase.

"Is Jayne dead? And the others who were in the cell with me? Are they all right?" She turned her eyes to him and he hated the frightened expression in their depths. "Sera said you sent the two who had philter home, is that true?"

"I did not," he stated. "It's not my duty to see to it, but they were sent back to Divinity unharmed. They were not suitable."

"And I am?" She gave a small laugh. "They didn't exactly interview us. They just looked in a cell and pointed at the two who were crying."

A measure of pride filled him. "You carried yourself well."

"So the others? Karre, Paige and Jayne?"

"Jayne we shall see in a few months and you can ask her yourself, but my brother would not harm her." Sorin silently added, *Unless he had to.* "Sir Aiden has taken Lady Paige to their home. Sir Vidar and Lady Karre reside near the battlefront at Spearhead. I am sure both ladies are well. We do not beat our women..." He lowered his voice and slipped his hand along her hip, daring to touch her and hoping she didn't shy away like in the hall. "Unless they ask us to."

She shivered but didn't jerk away. "I've been watching, listening, since I've arrived. I know you need women because you don't have a lot of your own. I know you made a deal with Divinity."

"Yea, we did. They approached us during battle. We almost slew them as allies to the Caniba."

Lilith slipped away from his touch and he felt an acute disappointment. Sorin followed her past the next cart of animal pelts, pointed at two soft furs, and motioned to the merchant. Not wanting the conversation to die, he told her about the first meeting with Divinity, the otherworlders' proposal for trade and assurance that they could find willing women who'd love to come to live at Staria.

The light clanking of a blacksmith drew Lilith's attention as she watched the man forge a blade. Sorin knew him well. Helmut produced some of the finest swords in all of Staria. He had several hanging on his weapons' wall.

"But they didn't tell us about it. They kidnapped us and sent us here." Lilith motioned toward the center of the market. Peasants continued to mill about, the busy sounds of their daily lives oddly comforting in their familiarity. "I've seen plenty of women who appear unattached. Why not marry one of them?"

"Unattached?" Sorin frowned, following her gaze. "Where?" He'd only seen three unattached females, but it would be years before any man thought of marrying them.

"Everywhere," she stated. Lilith looked around, finding a willowy sprite of a woman next to a group of five men. "There. She looks single and she's pretty. No wonder all five men are fighting for her attention. Why not seduce her with your power and rank? Or there, the dancing flower lady, I've seen her kiss three different men."

"They were her husbands," Sorin explained.

Lilith paled and she gasped. "You mean, I could have more than one husband?" She hugged her arms around her waist. "They could just come up and choose me?" Her eyes darted around the market, as if waiting.

Sorin tensed. "You wish for more—?"

"No!" she instantly denied. "I didn't ask for one husband. Is that why everyone keeps staring at me? Am I on the market, in," she gestured around, "the market? We have to go. I don't want some pig farmer jumping up and grabbing me. I highly doubt he has a high-tech facility like where I'm from. If you think I'm a wreck living in a castle, you don't want to see me on a farm. I don't do dirt or dung."

He relaxed somewhat amused by her reaction. "It's different with the peasants. The men choose, but are encouraged by the women who often take two or more husbands and never from the same family. Once a family is formed, they all have to agree before another man is let in."

"And there isn't jealousy?" Lilith bit her lip and scrunched her nose, instantly fascinated now that she wasn't being hunted by pig farmers. Sorin recognized her expression. She was analyzing and thinking again. What did she call it? Taking mental notes? Her constant curiosity didn't go unnoticed. The few times she'd talked to merchants it had been to ask detailed questions about their trade and their wares— how they were made, how long it took, how they liked living in a village towered over by a castle.

"It is necessity. The men need wives and poorer

families can live and work in larger numbers. This way, no one starves, everyone has shelter and families are protected. Those women who do not wish to marry choose a life of service following the armies. They're well taken care of and treated like queens."

"You mean whores." She nodded in understanding.

Seeing a knife with a pretty silver hilt carved with pictures of the forest, he picked it up and waved his hand to get Helmut's attention. The man kept working, hammering without watching his hands. Sorin indicated he planned on taking the blade. Helmut smiled and turned his attention back to what he was doing. Sorin handed the knife to Lilith. "I'll teach you to use it. Every woman should know how to protect herself."

"What? Running and hiding behind you isn't an option?" She laughed, taking the weapon from him. She pulled it from its sheath and examined the sharp blade. "I don't think my money works here."

"Why not? Mine does and what I have is now yours."

"Thank you. It's sweet." She glanced up and graced him with a faint smile before turning her attention to the gift.

By all the gods, he wanted to kiss her. Just

looking at her made his body tight from head to foot. Why wouldn't she reach for him? Didn't she want him as he wanted her? Even now he burned.

*Fool.*

*Idiot.*

*Weak.*

Sunlight illuminated the back of her long neck, as wisps of blonde hair escaped her upswept locks. He hesitated, but finally slid his arm around her waist to walk next to her. She didn't pull away. He clung to each sign of her acceptance of him.

"Tell me about Bianka."

Sorin dropped his arm from her, feeling as if she'd struck him. "There is nothing to tell."

"You know that's not true. What happened to her?"

"She's dead and her death is on my head. It was my duty to protect her, but I couldn't get to her in time." Sorin quickened his pace, forcing her to keep up.

"Did you care for her?"

"I told you, we don't give weight to such notions." Why couldn't she just leave the topic be? He didn't want to talk about Bianka, or think about her, or even remember her.

"Curse it, Sorin, you had to feel something. I can

tell you cared for her by the way you react. Call it what you like, but I think you loved her." She tried to grab at his arm. Peasants stopped what they were doing to watch the noble couple.

Sorin came to an abrupt halt. Glancing around, he saw they were close to the main road leading up to the inner bailey. He hooked her arm with his and guided her toward the gate. When they were relatively alone, he said, "You wish to know what I felt for her? Hate. Disappointment. Disenchantment. Her own people shoved her into a fairy ring to get rid of her. When I first saw her, I felt sorry for her. She looked like she needed protection."

"Sorin—"

He cut her off, continuing toward the gate. He kept his voice low so only she could hear and plastered a fake smile on his face for those who watched them. "Then her true nature was revealed. She was a selfish, cruel wench who demanded everything and gave nothing. When I left for war she tried to seduce the whole of my castle. When none would touch her, she burned down my home and ran away with every valuable she could fit onto her stolen horses. Nevertheless, she was my wife, and it was my duty to rescue her and keep her safe. I should have locked her in a tower. By the time I found her, she'd crossed over the Caniba border and propositioned one of their raiding parties. First, they took what she offered, then they took her valuables and her horses, and then they took her for food."

"Oh, Sorin, no."

He decided to take her to the brewery, knowing it would be empty and they'd have privacy. "I see the look on your face when I speak of fighting and my life, but there is a reason we are always at war. There is no peace with the Caniba. They are dishonorable, disgusting creatures. So as long as there is a Caniba and so long as there is a Staria, we will be at war. That is the role our gods have given us."

THOUGH STILL BRUSQUE IN NATURE, Sorin at least spoke. Lilith didn't know how to answer his tirade. When she thought his hesitance to talk about his late wife was due to emotional pain, it had been strangely imperative that she confront him. She had to make him face the truth of his loss if there was to be any hope of deepening their relationship. But this? His hard features and flat tone revealed not how much he could love, but how he could hate.

As they'd walked the marketplace, his hair dried

into soft waves. Cotton fabric molded to his strong body, stretching over his thick chest and muscular back. All day she did her best not to look at him too long. It had taken all her willpower not to touch him. But now, as he dragged her behind him, stiff and angry, a large part of her thought of running away and hiding in the surrounding town.

The market had been a wonderful experience, aside from the constant stares from the villagers. She did her best to pretend she didn't notice. Lilith loved studying their social interactions. It told a lot about the society to see their poor. Though, in truth, the poor didn't appear so poor. Everyone seemed to prosper. They were well fed, gave the impression they were happy, children ran around freely and not one beggar lined the streets in need of alms.

Sorin led her through the gate. Inside the inner bailey, soldiers practiced in the exercise field. They threw spears at distant targets, cheering good-naturedly when someone hit their aim, which apparently was often. Hurrying to catch up to Sorin as he strode toward a wide building constructed of wood, she tried to change the subject back to when he'd been talking to her without scowling. "So, none of the noblewomen take more than one husband? Is it illegal? Mind you, I don't wish for multiples, just asking."

He quirked a brow and directed her to follow him inside. The strong, stifling odor of fermenting liquor instantly filled her lungs. She blinked heavily, adjusting to the dim light as she coughed.

"Try not to breathe too deeply. They're malting the grain." He motioned to the side, but all she saw was a long stretch of material covered in what appeared to be dark sand over a smoker. Sorin took her hand and guided her through the first room. In the back, a narrow row of stairs led into the ground. The second room contained barrels of stored liquor, didn't smell as strong and had a chill to it. He turned a sharp corner, pushing into a third room. Light shone from a row of holes in the ceiling. Muffled noise from the exercise field filtered in. Despite the dirt floor and a single pale cobweb in the far ceiling corner, the place was empty.

"Where are you taking me?" The words barely escaped her when he tugged her into his arms.

"Right here." He stepped assertively forward, forcing her against an uneven stone wall. "I'm going to take you right here. No one will think to look for us in the cellar and I know you wish not to be seen."

Lilith saw the intent in his impassioned expression, felt it pressing unmistakably against her stomach. A shiver erupted along her flesh. The memory of his kiss caused her lips to tingle.

Deft fingers tugged at the scarf around her neck, parting it to expose the tops of her breasts. He squeezed her through the corset, moaning as eager hands worked a breast free from the top. Sorin pinched her nipple, following the hard caress with the softer suck of his mouth.

Lilith let out a weak cry. He devoured her with his hands and mouth, tugging at her skirt to lift it, slipping fingers next to his tongue so both could play with her nipple. Desire wet her pussy in anticipation. She helplessly explored his neck and shoulders, unable to do much else as he pinned her to the wall.

"I need to be inside you," he growled in animalistic urgency. "I've been hard since I woke up this morn, and your kiss in the hall only made the ache worse. All day I've pictured throwing you over the booths, taking you in the silky ribbons, on the fur pelts, over the hard iron latches."

It wasn't public and she knew no one could see them, but the sounds coming from outside, knowing so many people were close, caused her heart to quicken in what wasn't exactly repulsion. Sorin ran his hand up her bare thigh to her sex. He thrust a finger into the moist folds of her pussy.

"A-ah," he breathed hotly against her chest. "Please, do not deny me, my lady. I need you. If I don't find release soon inside your sweet body, I'll explode. Lift your legs around my waist. Let me inside you."

Lilith slid a leg to settle next to his waist. Sorin grabbed the other, hoisting her easily from the floor. She held onto his shoulders, gripping his tunic. Like a spear finding its target, he moved his shaft up her thigh. The thick tip of his cock head hit against her pussy, an instant reminder of how large of a man he was. His grip tightened on her hips and his eyes bore deeply into hers, as if to silently beg permission.

Lilith wiggled, circling her hips so she teased his arousal with the inviting wetness of her pussy. It must have been all the answer he needed, because Sorin lunged into her. Unlike the night before, he didn't ease his way into her depths. Instead, the full length of him glided to the root, burying itself in the tight sheath of her sex.

"Ah, I need to have you." As he said it, he pulled back and thrust again, hard and deep. "You're still so tight around me. I want to pound you until your pussy's the shape of my cock. I'm going to make you come so hard you'll never want another man between these soft thighs."

Lilith couldn't find the words to respond to his possessive decree. She'd never been taken so forcefully, so desperately, as if he'd die if he couldn't stake fast and hard claim to what he considered his. And as he jabbed wildly in and out, she couldn't think of one good reason why he shouldn't think that way. She was his, marked to her very core. Even if she left him, she'd never forget a single detail.

Sorin wasn't the only one whose desires had been building all day. Lilith met her release fast and hard, just like he promised. She tensed, panting and shaking as he thrust a few more times. Her legs went limp, the bones turning to tingling liquid. Sorin grunted, pressing her hard against the stone as he climaxed. He nuzzled her neck before letting her go. Her skirts fell about her unstable legs, and she stayed against the cool stones while she adjusted her bodice. Sorin pulled up his breeches, lacing them along the side of his hip.

"The hall should be ready to dine," he said, opening the door for her. She nodded, not meeting his gaze. He sounded so nonchalant. "It would be good for us to be there, together."

Lilith wound her hair back into the braids as she

left the ventilated room for the stifling brewery. As she stepped past, she expected Sorin to pull her into his arms and maybe kiss her temple, some sign of affection beyond the sex. His hand brushed the small of her back, guiding her along, but that was all.

"Have you considered the fire ceremony?" he inquired. "The weather is perfect for it, and it would be a nice gesture from the new noblewoman."

Lilith closed her eyes briefly. She didn't want to talk about a fire ceremony. She wanted him to kiss her head and say he cared for her. She wanted tenderness, affection. Hell, she wanted a hint at the possibility of love.

"I told Alana I'd speak with her tomorrow," she said flatly, not ready to give in to the bitch brigade who'd treated her like dirt before Sorin's public announcement.

"And tomorrow, what will you tell her?"

Lilith gave a small smile. "I'll probably tell her that I'll talk to her tomorrow."

## 10

LILITH STARED in amazement at her bed. Piles upon piles of trinkets from the market filled every corner until she realized that somehow each and every item she'd given so much as a sidelong glance at had been delivered to her room. There were bolts of fancy material, a wooden chair with a forest carved over the back, a sewing kit, woven baskets, ribbons and perfumes. A thick, silver-embossed book caught her eye and a tiny flutter went across her stomach.

Setting the knife Sorin had given her on the vanity, she walked around the bed. Pieces of leather rested atop fluffy white pelts. A wooden box filled with white candles butted up against a tall stack of blank parchment with feathery writing utensils and pots of colorful ink. There were silver goblets and chained necklaces such as she'd seen some of the women wear around the castle but had never really looked too closely at.

"Sorin?" she called, hearing someone move on the other side of the opened door. They'd just finished the eve meal and she'd come up before him —mainly to avoid more audience requests from the seemingly endless stream of women making their way to the head table. "I think there's been a mistake." She couldn't resist touching the book. Tracing the cover's edge, she lifted it open to peek inside. The language was nothing she could read without a translator unit and weeks of time. "I must have ordered things by accident when I was at the market. I didn't realize if you touched it you had to buy it."

"Accident?" Sorin appeared at her doorway, his heated gaze glancing over her before turning to the bed. She shivered at the unmistakably aroused attention. All through the meal he'd stared at her, touching his leg to hers under the table, pretending to bump into her hand whenever she reached for her goblet. "No, no accident. It looks like everything I ordered for you. If I missed something, let me know. Though, the maids should have put it away when I had them fill the tub. I'll send for Sera. They can work while we bathe."

He was out the door before she could protest his idea. Unwittingly, her gaze traveled to the bath and her skin began to tingle. His wet, gliding hands would feel pretty good against her flesh.

*It's not like everyone doesn't know what we're doing,* she reasoned, only to argue, *but that doesn't mean I have to flaunt it.*

When she heard the unmistakably steady beat of his footfall as he came back, she said, "You didn't have to get me all this stuff. I don't really need any of it. Well, I really like the paper and ink. And did you see inside this book? I think it's handwritten. I've never had a book like this." She continued leafing through the pages, desperately wanting to keep it. "Oh, and the perfume does smell really nice, but I have no idea what do to with iron hinges and raw leather."

"Ach, you are still clothed." Sorin stood in the doorway, naked. Her mouth fell open in surprise, not expecting it. He must have taken his tunic and breeches off in the speed of light as he crossed his room to get to her. "I had hoped to find you already in the bath." He strode to her, reaching to pull the scarf from her neck. "It is easily resolved. Unlace your corset. I have yet to look upon you naked and I plan to correct that without delay."

"The maids are coming," she said by way of denial.

Sorin groaned and leaned his mouth to claim hers, not caring that maids were on their way up and he was naked before the opened door to her room. He slanted his mouth to hers in a wondrously talented assault. When he pulled away, he rubbed his thumb between her eyes, smoothing out her wrinkle of concentration. "No, stop thinking about everything and just feel. No one cares what we do but us. I want to see you now. I want to feel every inch of you and give you pleasure."

Lilith found herself nodding, despite her logical judgment. His hands went to her bodice and pulled the stiffer material free. He pushed the corset down her hips, tugging it down to the floor. Outside the sky had darkened with late evening and firelight hit her from behind, casting her shadow across the floor. Next, he reached to pull the laces along her shoulder, unfastening the gown but not pushing it down her body. Warm hands ventured over her hair, undoing the braids so that the length fell free down her back.

"So lovely," he murmured. He stepped away, openly looking at her as he backed toward the fireplace. Taking an unlit torch from a basket on the floor, he pushed it into the fire and carried the flame toward the bathroom. All the while, he kept his eyes on her. His cock towered over his hips, already fully aroused and cast into stark detail under the bright torchlight. "Soft and sweet."

Lilith followed him to the bathing chamber. When she cleared the wall, he pushed on it, closing them in the smaller room and giving them privacy from the maids. Sorin hooked the end of the torch into a sconce carved in the wall. He stepped into the water and sat.

"Take off your gown. I want to see you." His arms spread over the back of the tub, as he watched intently.

She trembled under his full attention, but did as he commanded. Tugging at her shoulder, she let the material slip down her arms to reveal her chest and stomach. She pulled out of the sleeves and pushed the gown over her hips. Almost nervous, she stood, feet buried in her discarded gown. The chilled tower breeze hit her naked flesh and her nipples tightened in protest to the cold.

"Turn in a circle," Sorin ordered. "Slowly."

Lilith resisted the impulse to cover herself. Sorin's lids fell heavy over his eyes as she spun in a circle. When she made a complete rotation, she found Sorin with his hand on his cock stroking gently beneath the dancing orange surface.

"Come here," he beckoned.

Lilith stepped into the warm water, watching it ripple around her legs. Before she could sink into the tub, Sorin surged forward. Droplets trickled over his chest in captivating rivulets. He started at her toes, working up over her ankles, before his hands glided up the back of her legs to wet her skin. She sucked her bottom lip between her teeth, biting down.

She panted, a ripple of need coursing over her. His hands dipped down only to glide back up with the aid of the water. When he looked at her, she fell under his powerful trance. His will overtook hers and she knew she'd do anything he asked of her.

Sorin touched her flesh, rubbing delicately. His face was only a millimeter away from her stomach, his nose very close to nuzzling into her sex. She swayed on her feet, focused on the contact. Lilith welcomed the rush of sensations that his nearness brought. Hands moved along the intimate curve of her knee, tickling her with the lightness of their caress. Nestling his face intimately against the apex of her thighs, he inhaled, shamelessly reveling in her scent.

Lilith met his eyes, unable to fight the spell he wove over her. She trembled. Her pussy became very wet in a way that had nothing to do with the warm bath and everything to do with the sexy man currently worshiping her with his hands.

The torch reflected in his gaze, giving the piercing dark depths a mythical glow. Dark waves framed his face and she reached to brush the locks from his face. He closed his eyes and leaned into her palm, stroking her with his whiskered cheek. The thick muscles of his neck and shoulders shifted erotically with each subtle movement. He caressed her hips, squeezed her ass, licked a hot trail around her navel.

Then he did something completely shocking. He wrapped his arms around her and hugged her. The action was completely out of character for the great knight. Sorin's head pressed to her stomach and his hand splayed across her back as if he'd never let her go. Lilith trembled, about to stroke his hair when he released, continuing as if the moment never happened.

Throaty and raw, he whispered, "I want to bathe you."

He pulled back and she felt a chill without his touch. Lilith dipped down into the water, letting it lap against her shoulders. Nothing in this world seemed like it could be real, and she pictured herself strapped to a scientist's table somewhere being fed dreams while they probed her mind. The dark water reflecting torchlight, the handsome man who looked at her as if she were the most beautiful thing in all the dimensions, all of it had to be a dream.

"I don't want to wake up," she whispered. He looked at her questioningly and she blushed, realizing she'd said it out loud.

Sorin dipped his hands into a small jar left near the bath and rubbed them sensually together. Soap lathered between his palms. He stayed crouched in the water as he came for her with predatory grace. "Stand up."

Lilith obeyed. The long strands of her hair clung to her shoulders, glued in place as the water ran down her body. His firm lips set in concentration as he soaped her skin, gliding easily over her upper thighs, hips, ass and finally her breasts. She closed her eyes, enjoying the sensation of his touch. When she was alone with Sorin, she couldn't think or reason. All the dimensions faded away and there was only the two of them.

He stood, slithering along her flesh. The soap glided between them, an erotic caress, and she couldn't resist running lathered fingers over his arms and chest, washing him as he had her. They slid together, each caress a heady sensation. She liked the feel of him, the strength. He closed his eyes, moaning softly.

Sorin kissed her, working his mouth gently to hers. His hard cock pressed to her stomach. Fire shot through her senses, centering over her breasts and pussy. He tightened his hold and they sank into the bathwater. Sorin sat on the underwater stone ledge and tugged her onto his lap. Lilith straddled his thighs.

He looked deep into her eyes, forcing her to hold his gaze as he lifted her by her hips. The hard tip of his arousal, unyielding in its size, brushed her sex. She lowered herself onto him, impaling her pussy on the thick shaft. Sorin groaned, burying his face against her chest.

Lilith set the pace, tentatively at first, as she lifted up and down, up and down. He leaned back, giving her control. She grabbed his neck, holding onto his hair. The glow of firelight caressed every nuance of his bronzed flesh, giving texture to the many scars. Lilith didn't mind them, except for the hard life they represented. She felt bad for him and a little proud.

The slow, deep rhythm felt so good and weak

noises of pleasure escaped her throat. Her breasts bobbed before his face, drawing his avid interest. Lilith tried to make the feelings last, not wanting the terrific build of sexual tension to find release quite yet. But the more she rode him, the faster desire made her go until she found herself bucking wildly on his lap. Water splashed out of the tub, sloshing over the sides and onto the floor.

Lilith gasped, crying out as her climax hit her. She tensed, unable to continue moving as she stayed impaled on his cock. Sorin grabbed her hips, forcing her in shallow thrusts as he worked for his own release. He came soon after, joining her cry with an open-mouth yell of his own. For a long moment, she stayed on his lap with her head resting on his shoulder, breathing hard and willing her heartbeat to slow.

When finally she pulled back, insecurity filled her. Not because of what they did or how he was looking at her with a self-satisfied gleam to his gaze, but because as she looked at him her heart actually, physically ached. For the first time since waking up in Staria, she allowed herself to truly consider what it would be like to stay here, as his wife, for better or for worse, forever. The better would be these moments together. The worse would be the day the news of his death in battle would be delivered, and she would be expected to go to another husband.

Sorin moved beneath her and she slipped off his lap. Lilith dipped under the surface, rinsing off all remnants of soap. Sorin did the same before going to push at the wall.

"Wait," Lilith stopped him, brushing the wet locks from her face. "Are they still here?"

He glanced out into her room and shook his head in denial. "They are done."

Lilith stepped from the tub and reached to grab a folded linen. Their loveplay had wet the drying cloths. Before she could wrap the damp material around her body, Sorin lifted her into his arms. One hand wound around her thighs and the other behind her back. His fingers grazed the sides of her breast, skimming close to the nipple. The cloth dropped forgotten to the floor. He kissed her jaw as he walked her toward her bed. The maids had put everything he'd bought her at market away.

"Why the stone wall? Why not build a door?" Lilith asked.

"The builder claimed that in the winter it would provide better insulation in such a high tower." Sorin gave a small chuckle. "We all think he made a mistake of judgment, but couldn't admit to it because it is not the Starian way to rethink decisions."

Lilith had seen that Starian trait first hand. They definitely were a decisive people.

"That, or he wanted a place to please his wife and hoped the others wouldn't find out about it and think him weak. We were not always such a gentle people. Men did not always lavish their wives with gifts so openly, until someone discovered there were rewards to be had from a pleased mate."

Gentle? Lilith tried not to giggle at the concept. Lord Sorin might touch her gently, but she'd be hard pressed to call a warrior like him gentle.

He laid her on the warm, dry coverlet and stood by the bed. His eyes devoured her hungrily. "I should like to have you again, if you will allow me."

Lilith didn't know what to say, so she nodded in approval.

Sorin grinned, crawling next to her on the bed. Lying on his side, he cupped a breast, massaging leisurely before making a trail down her stomach. "So soft."

Lilith traced a long scar along his stomach. "So hurt."

Sorin glanced down the length of his body to

what held her attention. "It healed fast. I was only off a horse for two months."

Lilith found another scar and began tracing an oblong path around it. "I've been to these dimensions that are so medically advanced they can treat wounds like these in about two weeks, maybe even faster. They have lasers that do everything."

"Lasers?" He watched her finger find its next scar.

"Machines run with electricity." She frowned. How to explain?

"Ah, electricity." He nodded. "Divinity offered it to us when they saw our fires, but we have such knowledge. We find the torches better suited. Torch-light cannot be cut off by enemy spies."

That surprised her. She'd just assumed since they lived in the "Middle Ages", they *were* the Middle Ages. "But there is so much more than lights."

"What else do we need?"

"Medical lasers." She tapped his scarred chest.

"And who will make these lasers?" He leaned over kissing her neck. "You?"

"I don't know how." She shivered under his touch.

Sorin laughed. His fingers lightly brushed over

the soft curls guarding the slick folds of her pussy. The touch stayed light and teasing. "Nor do we."

She closed her eyes enjoying his exploring hands. Lilith tried to anticipate his movements, but it became impossible. His fingertips skated over her stomach, creating haphazard designs along her pelvic bone and up her chest. Tweaking a nipple, he made it erect.

Warm lips found her shoulder as he breathed against her. He encircled her clit, wetting himself in her cream. Lilith ran the back of her hand against his chest as she adjusted her hips on the bed to give him better access. The thick probe of his finger ran along her slit before thrusting inside.

"Oh," Lilith breathed, turning her face toward him. Her lips met with his forehead. The damp locks of his hair tickled her cheek.

One finger became two. Sorin moved within her, working in and out, faster and faster with each pass. Tension built. Lilith clutched at his hand, wiggling her hips as he brought her to climax.

Breathing heavily, she squirmed restlessly as he climbed on top of her. Sorin's body joined with hers. She wrapped her legs around the backs of his as he rocked inside her. Lilith moaned in encouragement. As his cock conquered her sex, his finger rubbed the hard bud of her clit. Wondrous sensations washed through her, and she couldn't believe she was coming again so soon.

Sorin's primeval grunt reverberated around her. His mouth opened wide and they both tensed in perfect unison. For a long moment they stared into each other's eyes.

Lilith yawned, every part of her relaxed. "I think I could sleep forever."

Sorin gave a small smile and nodded. He brushed his nose against hers. "Rest you well, my lady."

His weight left her. Lilith reached for him. But instead of lying down next to her, he stood beside the bed. Her hand fell short, hitting the air. Sorin strode from the bedchamber, going to his own bed. As he reached the door, he glanced back the second before disappearing.

Lilith sighed, a little hurt that he didn't stay. Was this what it was going to be like, a half marriage with a man who connected physically, but in no other way?

"Goodnight, my lord," she whispered, moving to hug her blankets.

## 11

LILITH STRUNG Lady Alana and her bunch of elitist snobs along for exactly eight days before finally allowing them to plan the festival. She still had no idea of what happened during the fire ceremony beyond the fact that there was fire, but Sorin insisted it would be good for her position as his wife to host it.

Now that people wanted to talk to her, she learned quite a bit about their lives at the castle—from how it ran so smoothly to the social hierarchy of the Staria system. Underneath the tough, war-focused exterior, it really was an impressive set up. They had a very "this is the way it is" attitude. Everyone had a job to do and they did it with little complaint.

Somehow, over the course of four weeks

following her trip to the market, more and more duties were given her. First, it was the audience—normally women seeking favors of some sort or wanting scarf-wearing fashion advice. Once, it was a knight trying to convince her to stop wearing the scarves so his wife would quit covering up her bosom. The old man's plea was so genuine that Lilith almost gave in to the request. Half the time Lilith got the impression they just wanted to talk to her so they made up excuses.

Next, they came to her with disputes—petty stuff that only required a mediator to announce the logical conclusion. Then they came to her for household decisions—what color to dye the next batch of bed linens, the upcoming week's menu approval—none of which she was properly trained to do. When she mentioned this, they brought her inventory of the larder and cold storage to help her decide. By the time Lilith realized she'd been systematically assimilated into the position of power she "married" into, it was too late to stop it. According to Sera, until a higher-ranking noblewoman came to the king's castle, Lady Lilith was in charge of all feminine concerns.

But then, there was her time with Sorin. Just looking at him made her forget whatever annoyances she had with her day. In the mornings, he'd take her out to the practice field to throw the knife he bought her. He wanted her to have a means to protect herself. Lilith was the first to admit knives were not her biggest talent.

After—and occasionally during—the lessons, he'd sneak her away to some private spot in the inner bailey and they'd make love. Sometimes he was hard and desperate, other times sweet and slow. Their evenings were spent in her bedchamber and her nights were spent alone. Sorin never once fell asleep by her side.

"Tell me about your home." Lilith glanced at Sorin next to her at the head table. He'd been quiet for days, even during sex, not that he was ever very talkative.

She still didn't like the watchful eyes of the others, but she'd gotten used to it. Poking at a strange brown and orange leafy salad, she pushed it aside. She wasn't the only one not eating it.

"Firewall?" He stiffened. She'd avoided talking about anything that hinted at Bianka, but it had been a month and her patience wore thin when it came to waiting for Sorin to volunteer information. "It is ash and rubble. Many of the villagers have moved away."

"Tell me about it before," she insisted. Lilith was

relatively sure he wouldn't yell at her in front of everyone.

"It was a fortress halfway between here and the borderland marshes, a last defense before Caniba armies storm Battlewar." Sorin dipped a piece of his bread and chewed.

"Was it a castle?" Did she have to stick a knife to his throat to get him to talk?

"Yea."

"Was it like Battlewar?"

"Smaller."

"Will you rebuild it?"

"Perhaps. Ronen wishes me to."

"Do you want me to finish you tonight?" Lilith put her hand on his thigh. Sorin tensed, his eyes rounding as he nodded once. It was the first time she'd ever taken such a bold initiative. "Then get used to having a conversation, my lord, or I'll lock my bedchamber door tonight. If you don't wish to talk about Firewall, then talk about something else. Just talk."

"The king sends for me to join the battlefront," he answered. "Sorceress Magda plans to lead her minions against Spearhead, a fortress near the marshland. Sir Vidar discovered her plot, and the king has sent for my army to reinforce Spearhead's knights."

"Is she really a sorceress?" Lilith trembled, seeing the serious line of his face.

"Yea. It is said she studies the black arts. Her followers dance with the serpent and are made to endure its poison before joining her army. Only those who live, the toughest of the Caniba, are allowed into her ranks, and those men live only to serve her with blind, obsessive loyalty." Sorin pushed his trencher of food away and grabbed a goblet of ale. "It's impossible to tell her numbers. Her armies live in the ground, hibernating like snakes. Most of our men who try to infiltrate her camp never come back. The others are never the same."

Lilith glanced out into the hall, noticing that several of the knights were just as stoic. It wasn't the ugly salad that put them off their appetites. They all knew what was happening. "I apologize for threatening you. I didn't realize you had so much on your mind. Why didn't you tell me?"

"You do not like hearing of war, and I do not like the disapproval on your face when I mention it. You always ask me about castles and people and food, but you never wish to hear about the realities of my life." Stormy eyes met hers.

"When do you have to go?" Lilith knew this day

would come, but she'd always found ways to distract herself from thinking about the reality of it.

"We march in the morning."

"The morning?" she gasped. "When were you going to tell me you were going?"

"Tonight." He set his goblet down and slipped his hand on her knee. "Or perhaps in the morning."

"How long have you known?"

"The king sent a missive."

Lilith jerked her leg away. "That doesn't answer my question."

"For some time." He didn't try touching her again.

"And you weren't going to tell me until you were practically riding out the castle gate?" She leaned into him, keeping her words low. "How long will you be gone? What if you don't come back? What am I supposed to do? I don't want to sit here and run a castle with nothing better to do than pine away for a man who may never return."

"What would you have me do, my lady?" His voice was calm, but the underlying current of anger was unmistakable. "Hide beneath your skirts like a coward? Send a missive to the king declaring I cannot fight because my woman disapproves and I shall forevermore be a farmer?"

"Excuse me, my lord." She stood from the table, trying to remain calm. "Please don't follow me. If you do, you'll not like the scene."

She strode from the room, fighting the nausea rising in her throat. Tomorrow? Not even twelve hours from now? What if he didn't come back? What if this was their last night together? Why in all the bloody Starian mace weapon things didn't he tell her this sooner? Because she made some kind of strange expression when she thought about him marching off to battle?

Lilith pulled at the red scarf around her neck, gasping for air. Her lungs constricted, as if she couldn't get enough oxygen. She'd seen the change in him, but only now did it make sense. He'd known he was leaving for days, possibly longer. The fantasy was coming to a swift end. She'd allowed herself to be swept into his gaze, telling herself that she still looked for a way home, but she hadn't really been looking. Not really. Not fully. Not like a woman who wanted her freedom.

She did want to leave, right?

Lilith took another deep breath. It didn't help. Did she go back to Sorin? Did she run? How long would he be gone? How dare he not tell her he was leaving her behind, in charge of a castle. Alone.

The sound of footsteps echoed on the Black Tower steps and voices carried from within the kitchen. Not wishing to see anyone, she ignored the stairwell and turned away from the kitchen. By now she knew her way around Battlewar Castle. Everyone would be at the eve meal leaving the sewing and laundry rooms abandoned. No one would think to look for her there.

Hurrying past the dungeon steps, she glanced down. Lilith stopped, taking a step back so she could get a better look. The door at the bottom had been left open a crack. Aside from each individual home above the hall, it was the only part of the castle she hadn't explored. She'd even been back to her old holding cell, though now it was empty.

Lilith ran her hand along the wall. The cold hard texture scratched her fingertips as she went to the thick door at the bottom. Expecting to see the surly Brock, she peeked through the barred window. The long, shadowed hall was empty.

Lilith glanced up the stairwell before hooking her finger around the edge of the door. She opened it slowly, trying to make sure it didn't squeak on its hinges. Rows of doors lined the long corridor. The first six on either side had bars, but the ones beyond that looked older with thick metal strips riveted across the front.

Her heartbeat quickened, so loud it echoed in the caverns of her ears, and she wondered what or who they had locked inside. Surely the Caniba people wouldn't be here, not the creatures whose name the Starians whispered like curses. Snake people who lived in the ground. Eaters of men. Monsters. Her natural curiosity forced her to move. Lilith took a deep breath, holding it as she crept up to the first door. There was only one way to find out.

Sorin nodded once as Brock appeared in the doorway to the main hall. The man's grim face told him everything he needed to know. Taking up his goblet, he couldn't bring himself to take a drink. A hard knot tightened inside his throat and his guts twisted, the sensation not unlike the moments before an unfavorable battle.

He'd agonized over his decision for days, but Lilith had to be tested. In the end, getting her to the dungeon door had been easy. Sorin was a master at strategy. Lilith wouldn't be able to resist exploring the unseen parts of the castle and an opened door to a sealed area would be all the invitation she needed.

The king needed him to march at Spearhead. Sorin needed to trust Lilith. He'd trusted Bianka and, the second he'd left her, she'd dishonored him and burned down his ancestral home. He could not make that mistake again. Already Lilith's reaction proved she wasn't happy about being left behind. Though, with her, he wasn't worried about her seducing other men so much as her leaving him forever. Two wives who didn't wish to be claimed by him? He shuddered to think on it.

The last few fortnights had been unlike anything he'd ever known. When he touched Lilith, he forgot everything but the feel of her skin and the look in her eyes. But not once did he imagine her to be content. He saw the way she thoughtfully looked over the distance. He heard reports of her endless questions to the servants. Had they seen any peculiar objects in the castle? Did they know how Divinity transported her there? No one told her anything and Lilith didn't yet have a clear picture of Starian loyalty, but that didn't stop her from trying to discover the truth.

What Sorin didn't know was, did her desire to know mean she'd leave him if she had the chance, or was it just her natural curiosity? He was sure he wouldn't like the answer.

*Fool.*

*Idiot.*

*Weak.*

Sorin watched the stoical nature of the hall. The men didn't know of his plan to test his wife and would think his mood due to upcoming battle. Tearing off a piece of bread, he forced himself to take a bite. Tonight, Lilith's true intentions would be revealed.

LILITH EDGED up to the door from her crouched position to peek through the bars. Tension rolled over her as she expected someone to reach out and grab her head the second it came into view. When nothing stirred inside the empty cell, she frowned and went to look inside the next ones. They, too, were empty.

*Who guards empty prison cells?*

Lilith wondered if they'd transported everyone out of there, or if perhaps they hid a more important secret. Her breathing deepened and she couldn't stop her legs from hurrying down the corridor in excitement. She tried the thick, metal doors, pulling them open. Some were weapon storage, crammed full of swords and shields, crossbows and maces. Others contained mining instruments and warm pipes that led up from the ground.

*There has to be more.*

As she neared the end of the corridor, she reached for the second to the last door and pulled. A soft blue glow came from within, very unlike anything else she'd seen at Battlewar Castle.

*Divinity.*

Lilith knew that light. She'd found the way home.

Inside, the blue glow lit her way as she hurried down a long row of stairs. They led deeper into the earth before opening into a large underground clearing. The cave's dirt matched what she'd seen on the mining instruments in the other room. At the end of the clearing, a large domed vault had been constructed to reflect the architecture of the castle. Every Divinity portal had a different look to it, but the main construct remained the same. A domed arch with a back and two side walls covered a center platform, their mass deceptively dense as to increase its own gravitational field and draw objects to it. The stone hid a complex configuration of liquid crystals, electrical currents, mirrors and vacuums. It was held in check by the wavelength of a specific blue light, which kept the portal inactive. Should the light change, a dimensional shift would occur taking whoever stood on the platform to a new parallel universe. In the early days, before the platforms, travel had been a haphazard affair, and many of the testers died by materializing inside solid objects. Now Divinity sent out microscopic probes first.

Once she found the controls, getting home would be easy. She'd simply send a long pulse of light color coded to her dimension and jump in. Though, on the other side, she'd find herself at Divinity headquarters in front of a team of their scientists. They might not be too happy with her return, but at least there would be plenty of witnesses there to see it. Maybe then she could get some answers. Maybe then she could help Jayne and the others and keep countless other women from being thrust into a strange world against their will.

Following the concentration of blue light to its source, a high beam shot from a high corner, she found the main controls mounted into the stone wall. Twelve turn dials indicated the color coding, including intensity and saturation.

Lilith hesitated as she stared at the dial. If she left Staria, she'd never be able to come back. Even if she got access to a portal, she didn't know the right code, and it was unlikely Divinity's directors would share the information once they authorized an origin reversal scan. She could portal jump for an eternity and never find her way back to Sorin. He'd be lost to her, forever. She didn't plan to make this discovery today, and it might be years before she could find her way back down the dungeon steps. She didn't even say goodbye.

How could she go?

How could she stay?

"I don't belong here," she whispered, trying to steel her nerves as she reached for the first dial. Turning them to the right settings was easy. She'd done it many times.

*Sorin's going off to battle. These people are not my people. I can't spend the rest of my life in this castle. After I learn all there is to learn, I'll have nothing to do but waste away. I can't live in one place, not knowing all the unexplored worlds that are out there. And I can't make this decision for just myself. The others need me to get help, to tell what Divinity has done.*

So many reasons to go—logical, good reasons. One reason to stay. She turned the seventh dial into position and reached for the next one.

"You chose to leave." Sorin didn't sound pleased as his voice echoed over the enclosure.

Lilith stiffened, making herself turn around to face him. "There is no choice, Sorin. I don't belong here."

"Somehow I knew you'd fail this test." An emotionless face stared at her, caressed by Divinity blue.

"You let me find this place." Lilith shouldn't have been surprised. It had been too easy—open dungeon door, empty cages, missing guards. She'd been so focused on discovery.

"Yea. I had to know if I could trust you when I was away or if you'd try to leave." He looked at the portal. "I see I have my answer."

"Let me go, Sorin. Let the others go. We don't belong here. We weren't given a choice. Please." She didn't try to finish dialing in the coordinates. There was no point. If he wanted he could easily stop her. The only way she was getting out of there now was by his good graces.

"You can choose to stay, my lady," he stated. After the intimacy they'd shared she hated to see that cold expression and tense body.

"No. I can't." She shook her head in denial.

"So be it." He sighed, his shoulder lifting under

the effort. "Then I shall decide for you. You will stay. Come."

"No," she said louder, praying she sounded brave and feeling incredibly weak. "I won't."

"I didn't ask." Sorin marched away from her toward the stairs, each movement taut with rage. Lilith reached for the eighth dial. Only five more to go. She clicked the next one into place. Sorin growled, spinning around to face her. He stormed across the clearing. Lilith flinched. He grabbed her arm and dragged her behind him. "I will not be betrayed again, Bianka."

"My name is Lilith, not Bianka," she corrected, noting the shaking in his hands and the fire in his eyes.

He blinked heavily when he looked at her and she saw the sway to his steps. He was drunk. "I will not be betrayed, Lilith."

"Is it so wrong to seek my freedom, my lord?" She tried to yank her arm from his grasp, but he only tightened his grip. Rage filled her at his heavy-handed treatment. "You claim Starians to be this noble race, so much better than the people you fight, but you kidnap women and force them to your will. What nobility is there in that?"

"I did not steal you, I chose you. You are my wife.

My honor could not take it if you left me." He quickened his steps, not saying another word as he met several of the guards at the top of the stairs. He nodded once at the group before hauling her back to the main floor of the castle.

*You are my wife. I could not take it if you left me.*

Sorin's fingers molded around the soft flesh of Lilith's arm, but she didn't cry out in pain so he didn't release her. He knew he drank too much ale at the eve meal. He felt the liquor flushing his face and heating his veins. Every thought echoed in his numbed head, forcing him to act on his most primal of instincts.

*Fool.*

*Idiot.*

*Weak.*

*Do not let her go. Force her to stay. She will be the ruination of me.*

Words tried to form in his throat, unfamiliar words, ones he would never allow to be spoken. He wanted to hurt her as she hurt him. His free hand balled into a tight fist, clenching and unclenching at his side. He wanted to reach into her chest and rip out her heart. He wanted to kiss her and touch her until she felt the passion he felt, the burning ache to be near her. He wanted her to think of him as he did of her, all the time, until the maddening need to just see her face and hear her voice were too much to take.

But she didn't feel that way. Her desire to leave him proved it. She didn't ache or burn or have a maddening need. Sorin couldn't imagine life without her, and Lilith didn't even care enough to tell him goodbye.

The pain hurt so badly he screamed, letting his voice roar over the hall as he pulled her to the Black Tower stairwell. He had to get her away from Divinity's portal, far away where she could never reach it.

"Sorin," Lilith said behind him, panicked. "You're scaring me. Let me go."

He stopped on the stairs, not even halfway up. With a swift pull, he brought her to his chest and held her tight. For all his pain and torment, he had to kiss her.

Lilith stiffened for a moment and he softened his touch. Her lips became pliable beneath his as she moaned softly into his mouth. With a hard push, she slammed him into the stairwell wall. His head banged against the stone but he barely felt it.

Like a woman possessed, she clawed at his clothing, scratching his flesh with her nails in her attempt to free him from his breeches. He enveloped her breasts in his palm, rubbing the globe until it slipped up and out of the corset top. Pinching the nipple, he liked the way it hardened between his fingers.

Lilith forced her hand down the front of his breeches, locking her fingers around his cock. She drove her hand up and down, fervently stroking him. Sorin couldn't focus beyond the taste of her lips or the feel of her hand. He wanted to shove himself inside her and slam his hips until he filled her with his seed.

Their bodies warred for dominance, continuing their earlier battle. She cupped his balls, rolling them. He inhaled a deep, ragged breath.

Sorin spun her around so her back was to him. Lilith gasped at the sudden movement as her hand was pulled from his erection. Clamping onto her hips, he forced her ass against his cock and groaned to feel the soft folds her gown padded by the firm line of her cheeks. He ground into her, undulating as she bucked beneath his hold.

Already she'd partially freed his cock and he made quick work of finishing the job. He clutched at her bodice, using the tight laces to control her. The length of her blonde hair tickled his fingers. Bending her forward so her ass arched toward him, he welcomed the vulnerability of her position. With his free hand he worked at her gown, lifting the skirts.

"You will feel me," he swore, desperate to make her understand his claim.

The smooth skin of her ass tempted his fingers and he splayed his hand over the warm flesh and squeezed. He rocked against her, letting the dry heat capture his shaft. Needing a wet ride, Sorin reached around to tweak the nub buried in the soft folds of her pussy. He knew how to rub her, how to make her instantly wet and ready. It didn't take much before the cream flowed freely between her thighs.

"You will feel my claim. You will know you belong to me." He barely heard the words, didn't care that they escaped his mouth. All that mattered was plunging inside her silken core.

Sorin pulled her over by her bodice so she had to support herself on the stairs. Then, taking her hips, he angled them up. Already the tip of his cock was wet with pre-cum.

The pink lips of her sex glistened with moisture. The erotic vision of his cock being swallowed into the folds made him bite his lip hard. He buried himself to the hilt. The tight muscles of her sex quivered and squeezed. Sorin took hold of the back of the corset to control her movements as he brought her back and forth on his cock, riding hard.

Lilith moaned, not fighting their passion. She let him have control, let him conquer with forceful thrusts. He let out an animalistic growl. Even in his anger over her betrayal, he couldn't get enough of her.

The sensations built. He wanted all of her, not just her body. Why in all the bloody wars of Starian history did she try to leave him?

Lilith tensed, her pussy clamping down on him as she came. Sorin answered her call, spilling his seed into her, hoping it took root. He wanted to fold her tight into his chest and never let go. Instead, he released her hips and fell back against the wall. The stairwell spun around him, and he had to close his eyes as he endeavored to slow his breathing.

"You will ride with us in the morn to Spearhead Fortress." Sorin couldn't let her stay behind. To give orders to have her watched would be humiliating, and he couldn't leave her unattended so close to Divinity's portal.

"You're never going to let me leave, are you?" Lilith asked, her soft voice hurting him worse than a dagger to the gut.

When he opened his eyes, she sat on the stairs, looking up at him with her damning blue eyes. She'd righted her clothing, but the tousled hair and flushed cheeks showed all signs of their shared passion. Sorin answered the only way he could. "No, my lady, I will never let you leave."

Lilith didn't speak as they rode from Battlewar. When she told Sorin she couldn't ride, she hadn't lied. Straddling a giant horse as it nervously pawed the earth, she'd spent all of one minute on the creature's back before Sorin ordered a cart with blankets so that she may be pulled behind the traveling band of knights.

The cart suited her better than the animal, as she rested in the back, curled around a blanket and praying the bumpy trip would be a fast one. She hugged her hands to her chest, cuddling beneath the covers. Her palms were raw from gripping the stairwell. At the time, she hadn't noticed, too caught up in Sorin's violent possession.

How could she have thought of leaving him?

How could she think of staying?

The sound of pounding horse hooves echoed on the prairie, trampling the tall grasses as they made their way to a forest path. Lilith moaned, pulling the blanket over her head to block the sunlight. When Sorin said they'd leave in the morning, he hadn't been lying. He had her awake and packed before the sun even rose.

"So close," she whispered, thinking of the portal. If she hadn't hesitated, she would be home demanding answers. The "why" bothered Lilith more than anything else. Part of Divinity's creed was never to play god.

"Are you ill?"

Lilith pulled the blanket off her face. Sorin rode beside her cart and from her angle he seemed a giant, towering beast of a man. "I didn't sleep well."

His mouth pulled into a straight line and he turned his eyes forward. "Signal if you have needs."

He rode off and Lilith pulled the covers over her head once more. Right now her most pressing need was sleep.

AFTER THREE HORRIBLE days inside the jerking cart, suffering from aching muscles, stomping horses and a husband who barely said more than ten words to her, Lilith had never been so happy to see a castle in her life. Though nothing compared to the great city of Battlewar, Spearhead had a quaint charm—for a fortress on the brink of a vicious Caniba attack.

A single tall watchtower lifted into the sky, lording over the square-shaped castle beneath. Thorn hedges formed a perimeter around the outside wall, surrounded by the murky waters of a moat. As they passed over a bridge to the opened front gates, Lilith swore she saw something swimming in the water. The raised stone of the bailey wall surrounded the courtyard, looping about from one side of the main castle to the other in an oval shape. Atop the wall that stood several feet wide was the walkway surrounded by battlements with corner spiral stairwells leading from the ground to the battlements. Next to the tower, the main part of Spearhead Fortress sprawled along the backside of the wall.

Shadows fell heavy over the wide courtyard and a gentle evening breeze flitted over them. Spearhead guards pushed the oversized doors of the main gate closed and latched them with a thick timber. A couple of women hauled baskets heaped with laundry, while others carried water buckets from the well.

"I see you've survived," a female voice yelled as Lilith's cart came to a stop. "I had my doubts."

Lilith crawled out of the cart, rubbing her aching back as she tried to force her numbed legs to stand. A loud, ear-splitting whistle resounded over the yard. Lilith jerked, turning to the noise. Karre stood bound to a t-shaped post in the middle of the courtyard. A chain ran along the top, binding her wrists over her head and a large shackle held her waist to the post, leaving her feet free to kick at the dirt. Smiling, the woman waved her fingers, causing her chains to jingle at the movement.

"Great weather we're having," Karre said conversationally, smiling as if she sat down for a fancy evening with the ladies. Lilith glanced around the yard. Sorin's dirt-covered knights and equally caked horses hardly qualified as fancy.

Seeing her husband talking to a group of men, Lilith walked toward the woman, wondering if anyone was going to stop her. No one did. She lowered her voice to ask, "Karre? Are you all right? What's happened here?"

"Small misunderstanding." The woman gave a

derisive laugh. "Nothing to be concerned about. How's your guy been treating you?" Karre leaned to the side, studying the newcomers. "Which one was he again? The big guy?"

"I found the way out. It's at Battlewar Castle in the dungeons," Lilith whispered. Karre's easy smile dropped and her eyes narrowed. "I tried to leave to bring back help, but it's too guarded."

Okay, so it wasn't a complete lie. There was no reason to say she hesitated and got caught in Sorin's trap, that he let her find it to test her.

When Karre didn't answer, Lilith continued, "Have you seen Jayne or Paige?"

"No. You're the first." Karre's smile lifted somewhat, though her eyes stayed focused in concentration. The expression appeared to be more for show than a real emotion.

"I promised Jayne I'd try to get word to everyone. I'll draw you a map and write down the code to my home dimension. I'll find a way to get it to you, just check your chambers. Someone at Divinity headquarters should help anyone who comes through the portal if you tell them what happened. If you see Jay—"

"Sh." The single, quick syllable cut her off.

Louder, Karre announced, "Yep, beautiful weather for a ride into battle."

"My lady," Sorin said behind Lilith. She wasn't sure which "lady" he spoke to, so she didn't answer.

"My lord." Karre bowed her head, the action mocking when done with rattling chains. Lilith opened her mouth to speak, hoping to reassure the poor woman. Karre cut her off when she began to hum a playful tune as if she hadn't a care in the universe.

Sorin took her arm and led her from Karre. The knee-length flaps of his black long tunic brushed against her. His faster gait caused her to stumble and swing back as he held her tight. He stopped and she caught herself.

"You look pale." Sorin placed a finger beneath her chin and lifted her head.

"Just tired. The horses didn't stop and I'm not accustomed to sleeping in moving carts." Her neck muscles twinged and she turned away from his touch to get more comfortable. Though, in a way, she was happy for the aching muscles. They had distracted her from the ache in her chest and loins. Seeing Sorin, so thick and proud, astride his giant horse did things to a woman. Had they been alone she might have jumped from the cart and knocked him to the ground to have her way with him.

"The speed was necessary," he said. "Sir Vidar sent word that we were to hurry."

They stood in the courtyard, surrounded by the bustle of the newly arrived guests. Horses were led away by young boys. Servants welcomed the men, ushering them inside. Friends greeted friends.

"Was that the rider we met two days ago?" Lilith remembered seeing the rider, but no one had told her anything. As the only woman on the voyage, she'd been lacking in conversation. Though she did over-hear a very inappropriate conversation about hanging genitals and severed heads.

"It was." He nodded.

"I wondered." She hoped to keep him talking, but already she felt him slipping away.

"You should have asked." Sorin took her arm, gentler than before, and led her inside the keep. Though like Battlewar in concept, the main hall was smaller and lacked all decorations.

"What's happening to Karre? Why is she tied up?" Lilith asked when they found seats at the high table.

"A misunderstanding," a deep, resonate voice

answered, leaving no room for further questioning. The knight bowed toward Sorin, acknowledging him before doing the same to Lilith. She nodded once, struck by the strangeness of his hazel eyes. Flecks of gold gave them an animalistic property.

"Lady Lilith, may I introduce Sir Vidar." Sorin motioned to the man. "This is his home."

"Only until the king assigns it to another," Vidar answered. "My lord, if you would come with me?"

Sorin looked as if he'd touch her, but instead he merely turned to follow Vidar, leaving her alone at the head table. Feeling a whole new set of curious eyes examining her, she tried to smile for the people of Spearhead. They did not smile back.

"Did you find out why Karre's been chained?" Lilith sat on Sorin's bed in the small guest chamber, her eyes on him the second he opened the door as if she'd been waiting for him to arrive. "Sorin?"

He sighed at Lilith's panicked question. When would she learn that the Starian men did not harm their women? What business was it of his if Lady Karre enjoyed being tied in the courtyard? Had she actually been abused, most likely the people of Spearhead would have revolted against Sir Vidar in protest.

"I did not ask," he said honestly. Weary from a long evening pouring over maps and organizing the armies, all Sorin wanted to do was rest. Well, resting wasn't *all* he wanted to do. He could think of at least a dozen other things that all included his wife naked and impaled on his cock. However, after his drunken blundering in the stairwell, he couldn't bring himself to touch her. "It is between Vidar and his wife."

"What did you talk about, then?" Lilith made no move to go to her own adjoining room. "Your war?"

Sorin pulled at his boot, flinging it aside in frustration. It wasn't *his* exclusive war. He didn't lie in bed at night thinking of ways to start battles—at least not often. "It's been decided that we ride south at dawn to join an encampment of soldiers not far from the borderland marshes."

Lilith moaned, rubbing her neck. "Do we have to leave so soon? I haven't recovered from the last journey."

"You will remain here." He tossed the second boot and rolled back on the bed, his feet planted on the floor. "It is too dangerous. Sorceress Magda has yet to show herself, but they found tracks near the marshes. It's not safe for you at the encampment."

"You want me to stay here alone?" She crawled to sit close to his head and look down at him. Blonde hair framed her, cocooning his vision so all he could see was her face.

"A small contingency of soldiers will be left behind to guard the fortress. They will protect you."

"You can't leave me here," she insisted, her eyes widening. "I don't belong here. These—"

"You keep saying that, Lilith, but you do belong here. I'm here. You're my wife and I want you close." He closed his eyes, unable to keep looking at her without touching her. Three days without her body next to his had been too long.

"Don't you mean you want me prisoner?" The bed shifted and he felt her pulling away from him.

"No," he stated flatly. "You made your choice. You cannot be trusted to remain at Battlewar. Had you not tried to leave, I would have let you remain there."

"Sorin, can't you understand? I've spent the last three days trying to think of how to explain it to you. It's not that I want to leave you." She pushed up from the bed and began to pace. "You have your job, your war, your life here. I'm nothing. I hate approving menus. I hate being asked which color of linen to put on the beds. My idea of a décor is leaving stacks of books on the floor next to my bed. I can't stand listening to two women fight over who saw a trinket first at market, and I definitely don't want to be the one to decide who should get it." He watched her agitation grow, not knowing what to say. "I want to learn things. I want travel to other dimensions. I love my job. I love the books and the scrolls and the meticulous research. I love observing other cultures. I miss pasta and pizza and room temperature controls. I miss pullovers and cotton pants. I miss," she shrugged helplessly, tossing her hands to the side, "so much."

He clenched his teeth, not liking her words but respecting their truth.

"And I'm sure it's the same for the others. If you force us to stay, then we're nothing more than slaves you traded minerals for." She stopped pacing and stood before him.

Sorin hated the look in her eyes, the desperate pleading for him to understand. He understood, but how could she ask it of him? How could he let her go? Forget what it would do to his reputation and honor. How could she expect him to go on without her? Every instinct told him to cling to her, to force her to care for him. He was a man of action and power. He bent men to his will with the force of his reputation proven in battle. His reputation didn't impress her. Nothing about him impressed her. So, how could he make her stay without force? Never before had he been so conflicted. He knew right, but every part of him begged for wrong.

"Don't say anything now." She came back to the bed and sat next to him. "I know what I ask conflicts with your culture, but please consider it."

He nodded once, not speaking.

Lounging beside him, she ran her hand over his heart, first tracing the red crest on his chest before following the valleys of his muscles down to his flat stomach. "Thank you, Sorin."

He refused to move as she pulled at his tunic, working it up over his thighs. Then, dipping her hand beneath the thick black fabric, she continued her teasing caress along the flesh of his abdomen. Her fingers felt cool compared to his body heat.

Lilith concentrated on the movement of her hand, watching the bump it made under his tunic. Sorin drew his hands behind his head, eager to see what she'd do next. Normally he was the one to touch her, seduce her. His breathing deepened. A delicate fingertip traced his navel before sliding up the center of his stomach. His tunic stopped her progress and she had to change routes, moving along his side to his hip.

"You're always so warm," she whispered thoughtfully. "It's like you burn a couple degrees hotter than everyone else."

His cock pressed against his breeches, lifting them visibly.

"Maybe you do," she continued, her fingers becoming heavier against him as they glided down to cup his growing erection.

LILITH HELD his tunic as she brushed feathery kisses across his stomach. The familiar smell of him filled her head, potent and raw and so very male. Everything about the way he moved, looked and tasted bespoke of something primal. Unable to resist, she drew her tongue over his flesh, eliciting a small groan from Sorin.

She held his cock in her hand, marveling that it could already be so hard and ready for her. Her body became wet in response. Small, animalistic noises escaped him as she continued to stroke and kiss. He shifted as he reached for his waist to tug at the laces along his hip. The material beneath her massaging hand loosened to give her a better feel of his shape.

Sorin put his hand back behind his head, letting her have her way. She kissed harder, biting and licking along his hipbone. The faster she rubbed his heavy arousal, the more his breeches bunched. They pulled down to expose the tip of his cock. The mushroomed head was so close, so smooth and tempting. Her lips willingly answered the call, opening wide so her tongue could lick a torturous trail along the ridge joining salty tip to thick shaft.

His body shifted and his hips rose from the bed. She kissed the tip, rolling her tongue down the length of his shaft. He jerked and moaned, clearly past the point of going slow. Hands delved into her hair, pushing her down to take him deeper.

Lilith braced her hands on the bed to keep him from pushing her down too far. As she sucked, his grip lessened and he let go. She rolled his balls in her palm gently. Her entire body tingled and ached. She didn't want to think about anything beyond this moment.

"Come here." Sorin groaned. Taking her by the arm, he pulled her off his arousal and up his body.

Lilith lifted her skirts and straddled his waist, as Sorin made quick work of her corset top. Warm hands slid up her gown to cup her breasts, pinching and rubbing the nipples until she writhed on top of him. Her pussy ached, wet and needy, ready to be dominated by the handsome warrior beneath her. There was an urgency to their touches, a desperation that hadn't been there before. She couldn't help thinking this might be the last time they were together. What if he didn't come back from battle? What if she never felt the touch of his hands? Saw the steamy glaze to his passion-laden eyes? Or felt the confident thrust of his body in hers?

Lilith gasped, torn between the momentary pleasure and the unexpectedly deep pain that racked her heart. How could she have thought of leaving him? Just the thought of never seeing him again tore at her chest until she wanted to scream with the agony of it. She closed her eyes tight, fighting back the bittersweet tears, not wanting him to see her cry.

*I love him.*

The thought she'd been trying to suppress since first she saw him came surging forth.

*I love him. I love Sorin. Don't go tomorrow. I won't be able to take your leaving.*

There was no point in saying the words out loud. He didn't put stock in love. He was a warrior. Her warrior.

She lifted up, all inhibitions gone. She wanted him inside her, needed to feel their connection. All thoughts left her at the intimate brush of his arousal. Three days had been too long a time to go without him.

Lilith pushed down, impaling herself on his length. The thick probe stretched her wide, forcing her to go slow as she fitted him inside her. Once deep, she moved her hips in small circles, rocking around and around, hitting that sweet spot of pleasure inside her pussy.

Sorin grabbed her thighs beneath the gown and held on tight. He lifted her up, controlling her as he slammed her down hard only to let her lift up once more. Lilith rose above him only to have him jerk her down as he arched off the bed to meet her thrust for thrust.

She gripped his hands through the material, enjoying the wild ride. Suddenly, she tensed and fell forward, shaking with release. Tremors erupted all over her body, making her limbs weak. Her heart raced, pounding so loud it echoed in her ears. Sorin bucked beneath her, growling as he held her flush against his cock. He jerked in violent climax.

When he let go, she fell next to him. Neither of them moved, as they lay with disheveled clothing and limbs sprawled at odd angles. Sorin breathed heavily next to her, the harsh sound holding her attention.

Lilith didn't want to love him. What did she know about loving a warrior in a primitive land? This place wasn't her place. She hadn't lied to him about that. She hated directing servants and all the other things a Lady of Staria was supposed to do.

*But Sorin is here,* her heart argued. *What does all the rest matter if you get to have him?*

Sorin's hand brushed her cheek softly, drawing her gaze to meet his. "Good eve, my lady. You rest. I will take the other bed."

Lilith reached out, grabbing hold of him to keep him from leaving. "Don't go."

Surprise filtered over his face. "You wish to do it again. I thought you were exhausted from our journey." Though obviously tired, he looked willing.

"No, you need rest."

Sorin's surprise turned to confusion and he nodded before starting to sit up once more. "Very well."

"Stay," Lilith said when he would leave. She pulled on his arm. "I wish for you to stay with me." He lay back down. Lilith let go and climbed up the bed to crawl under the covers. He turned his head, angling his neck so he could watch her. She patted the pillow next to her. "Sleep."

"Together?"

"Yes, my lord, together. Sleep." She again patted the bed. He pulled out of his clothes, tossing them aside before joining her under the covers. Lilith tried to close her eyes, but felt his attention on her and finally opened them.

Resting on his side, his arm bent under his head, he studied her. "I have never slept with another in my bed." Lilith would have giggled at the admission, except that he looked so serious telling it. "It is not done except in poor homes."

"And what is the reasoning for that?" She ran her hand over the bulges in his arm.

"Women normally demand their own space, so that we husbands do not take too many of our husband rights. Additionally, if there is an attack, the ladies will be safer away from the main door to the bedchambers."

Lilith did giggle that time. She couldn't help it. "That has to be the sweetest reasoning, though I think I am safe enough next to you." She laughed harder. "I thought it was because I snored that you kept leaving my side."

"I have never heard you," he assured her. "So, where you come from, is a shared bed the custom?"

"Yes, it is." Lilith felt giddy. This was perhaps one of the very rare times he asked about where she came from.

"I cannot do anything about our station, Lilith, but I will speak to the servants. I do not want you to hate your life here, but please understand, I can't let you go." He didn't touch her and she let her hand slide from his body.

"Why?" Lilith held her breath. *Say you love me.*

"You know that answer. Honor. Duty. Tradition. Reputation. You are my wife. We belong to each other."

*Say you love me.*

He didn't.

"We should sleep," Lilith said, trying not to choke on the words. "You have to ride in the morning."

"I will do right by you," he persisted.

"Good night, Sorin." Lilith closed her eyes and pretended to go to sleep, telling herself that at least this time he stayed.

Sorin did not want to leave his wife. Her gentle presence throughout the night had soothed him, and he'd slept deeper than he could ever remember. Perhaps it was knowing she was so close at hand, that all he had to do was reach out and touch her to assure himself that she hadn't left him.

However, as he looked down at her sleeping form, over the flushed warmth of her cheeks, the long line of her neck exposed by tousled blonde hair, he shivered. In the early morning hours he couldn't fool himself with dreams. She didn't want to be here. If he hadn't stopped her, she would have left him. She would leave him still.

He didn't like the fear he felt in going off to fight. Never had he hesitated when riding off into battle, not even the cold wintry morn of his first bloody fray as an untried youth. It wasn't the sword or even death that frightened him. It was the thought of Lilith finding a way to leave him and never coming back.

How could he live without her?

How could he breathe?

Even now his chest constricted. Damn honor and reputation and pride. He wanted her to stay. Sorin reached out to touch her, intent on shaking her awake and demanding she never go. His knee hit the bed and she sighed, her head turning. The soft action stopped him. Everything about her seemed so fragile. He clutched his hand into a fist and backed away.

"I will fight well. I will make you proud, my lady," he whispered. It was the only thing he could think to say. Everything else jumbled in his mind, unable to find the right words or expression. "Upon my death, I will honor you."

SORIN LIFTED HIS SWORD, slashing and hacking his way through the throng of hairy, man-eating beasts. The Caniba warriors all looked the same to him—smelly, pelt-covered monsters with sunken eyes and sharpened teeth. Their hair hadn't seen a comb, ever, and he highly doubted any of them had heard of bathing.

Rumors flew that these creatures weren't men, but beasts created from the fornication of people and ancient wolves. Sorin had killed plenty of them to know that they were of flesh and blood. They had the bodies of men, but were the basest example of what men could become. He doubted the noble wolf sired them, but he did not doubt for a second that they were truly beasts.

Three days earlier, Sorceress Magda's army had come up from the ground right through the middle of their encampment. Like a giant serpent of dirt snaking through the ground, the topsoil had sucked into a pit taking a few of their men with it. Caniba warriors rose up, splitting the Starian army in half. Sorin's half was surrounded and fighting an army twice their dwindling size with little reprieve.

Sorin thrust his sword into the stomach of his enemy, watching the beast's gnarled face remain impassioned as if he didn't feel death. He'd seen the same look many times. The Caniba felt nothing beyond a driving need. Sorin spun on his heels and withdrew his blade just as quickly as it went in. Yelling to release the tension of battle, he swung once more and beheaded a blood-soaked figure.

The smell of sweat and dirt and death filled his nose. Metal clanged, men screamed and moaned and died all around him. Sorin knew these horrors well, but this battle was different. Try as he may, he couldn't keep Lilith out of his head. He saw her disappointed gaze staring at him from the corner of his eyes. Her face appeared in swirls of kicked up dust and her tears in droplets of blood. She would not be pleased with what he did. His honorable deeds would not make her proud.

Sorin fought harder, driving through the throng. He needed to get to her and hide her from the truth. If she discovered his deeds, if one of the men sang his praises not knowing her heart, Lilith would run.

*Just like Bianka. No, never like Bianka.*

"Argh!" Sorin swung his arm, the movements as natural and practiced as walking.

"To Lord Sorin!" a cry went out over the field, only to be repeated. "Follow my lord, he's going for the Sorceress!"

Sorin glanced over the battlefield, his vision hampered by dust. Before him he saw the makeshift throne of Sorceress Magda. Eerily pristine in her gown of sparkling white, she sat on a carved wood platform, lifted up so that she might watch the carnage she'd created with the pride of a goddess. Dark, smooth hair fell about her shoulders to her waist, and the inky depths of her eyes became even more so by the black lines drawn thick around them. Right now, that bloodthirsty gaze was on him. Her evil children swarmed around her, a thick, living wall of protection.

He realized he'd fought his way close to her, closer than they'd been the entire battle. Sorin had been so distracted by thoughts of Lilith that he'd broken rank, leaving the tightly formed unit of knights behind him. Caniba soldiers turned their attentions to him.

"To Sorin!" the men shouted. "To a good death!"

"Forgive me, my lady," Sorin whispered in response to their cries. There was no way he could fight his way to kill the Sorceress, and by the gleaming pleasure of her expression she knew it as well. He had one chance and he was going to take it. For Staria, for Ronen, for family honor and for Lilith, though she would not appreciate the deed, he arched back and threw his main line of defense. The sword flew through the air, singing toward Magda.

A swarm fell on him, blocking his view. Teeth bit into his forearm, as he grabbed the knife from his waist. The weight of thronged bodies pushed him to the ground, and all his strength and training couldn't stop it. Burning, white heat filled his arms while sharp, metal-tipped nails clawed into flesh. The foul Caniba smell encased him.

*I fought well, my lady, take pride in that.* Sorin thought, hacking the best he could with restrained arms. *Upon my death, I honor you.*

THE SOUND of the gate caused Lilith to jump from her seat in Spearhead Fortress' main hall. She'd grown to know it well in the two weeks she spent waiting for Sorin's return from battle, and each time it drove the stake of fear deeper into her chest. How could he go without waking her? Why didn't he send word?

*I should have made him promise to come back. He would have kept his word.*

Panicked, she tried to act nonchalant as she walked through the aisle of tables to the door. Karre had disappeared that first morning, and someone told Lilith the lady rode to battle with her husband. It had been an easy enough task to find Karre's chambers and hide directions to the portal. She only hoped a servant didn't find it first.

Knights came and went, always armed and covered in blood as they rode into the castle, always grim-faced and determined when they rode out. A few times she'd seen them walk to a random woman in the yard to present the sword of a fallen husband. Most accepted the dark gift with a nod and stiff retreat. One woman screamed and fell to her knees, shaking and grasping the blade as if she'd end her own suffering. No one moved to stop her, but in the end she merely curled into a ball and lay in the muddy earth. Lilith had stayed back at the glare of a guard warning her not to interfere.

What if she was next? What if it was Sorin's blade they presented to her?

*I can't take this. Please, make it stop. I can't take it.*

As she stepped into the evening sunlight, she pressed a fist to her chest. The unknown was slowly killing her. She'd barely eaten. The smallest of sounds would cause her to jump out of her skin, and every moment became a worry-filled piece of hellish agony.

The sound of horse hooves greeted her as a single rider passed through the gate. Guards hurried to close it as soon as he'd cleared the large doors. Lilith stumbled to a halt, instantly seeing the extra sword sticking from the pack on the man's horse. She knew that hilt, that blade. She'd seen Sorin clean it after their morning knife-throwing lessons.

"No." Lilith shook her head, backing away from the man, willing him to disappear, to not see her. If he didn't hand it to her, it wouldn't be true.

The knight's eyes scanned the courtyard before finding Lilith. She froze. He didn't look away. Why didn't he look away? The sword had to be a replica of Sorin's. It couldn't be his.

Tears filled her eyes, blurring her vision. She blinked hard, trying to keep her world from spinning in circles. The hall behind her had gotten eerily quiet. People no longer moved about the yard. Why were they looking at her?

*Look away! All of you. Stop it.*

The rider dismounted, his actions seeming both fast and slow at the same time. By the heavy breathing of his mount, he'd ridden hard to get to Spearhead Fortress. His brown hair slicked back from his head, plastered into place by sweat, and his face carried the same grimness the others bore. She didn't recognize him.

Lilith grabbed her stomach. Taking the sword from the pack, he revealed the broken blade. The metal had been snapped in two.

Hot tears spilled down her cheeks, sliding down her chin to drip onto her scarf. As the knight neared, she clutched her stomach harder, grinding her fingers into the hard corset to stop its ache. She tried to break the connection of their gaze, but his eyes kept her steady. Hands lifted to give her the sword, and she saw dried blood still caking the remaining blade. Lilith shook her head in denial.

"No," she whispered, barely able to make the word leave her throat.

"My lady, I—"

Lilith didn't give him a chance to finish. Bile rose, making its way up her body and out her mouth. The knight jumped in surprise as she threw up on the front of his tunic. The broken sword fell from his hand, hitting Lilith's skirt and snagging the dark blue material.

"By the rotting marshes, my lady," the man swore.

"Cedric!" a stern voice charged. Sir Oskar had command of the fortress in the absence of Sir Vidar. "You will not swear at Lady Lilith or upset her."

Cedric's brow furrowed as he looked at his stained clothes.

"All know she is with child," Oskar announced.

That brought her head around. "What?"

"It is quite all right, my lady. We noticed your pallor, refusal to eat aught but pieces of bread, the restless wandering at night, and your nausea confirms it." Sir Oskar gentled his look as he spoke to her. "Cedric should not have alarmed you with news of war without talking to me first. Lord Sorin asked us to look after you, to make sure you were comfortable and not bothered with talk of battle. We came to understand quickly his reasons."

Lilith shook her head, utterly confused. She

wasn't pregnant. She couldn't be. Turning to the more horrific matter of the sword at her feet, she asked, "What happened? Can I see him?"

At the news of her "condition", Cedric calmed his temper and he began tugging out of his tunic. "Lord Sorin honored your family name, my lady. He fought well against the Sorceress's army."

She touched her stomach. A baby? A piece of her husband to carry with her? If only...

At their expectant looks, she nodded weakly. Inside, she felt numb. "I'm sure he did. He's a very good soldier."

Cedric dropped his tunic on the ground before reaching to take the broken sword. He again tried to give it to her. Lifting his voice so all those gathered could hear, he announced, "With this blade Lord Sorin injured the Sorceress Queen, proving she's mortal and bleeds like the rest of them."

Cheers erupted. Lilith flinched, wanting desperately for them to shut up. The sound echoed in her head.

"I present it to you, my lady, to honor you and your child." Cedric bounced it in his hands.

How could she touch it? "Where is he?"

"At the encampment. He asked that I bring you to him," Cedric answered.

"Bring me...?" she repeated, breathless. "But, how could he ask? Are you saying he's not...?" Lilith didn't dare hope.

"My lady?" Cedric prompted.

"He's not dead?" Lilith looked at the broken weapon.

"No, my lady."

"Then why in the blasted stars are you bringing me this?" Lilith slapped at the hand holding the sword, making him drop it. She screamed in anger, releasing some of the pain he'd caused her with his little show of presenting the sword. The weapon dropped and Lilith swung at the man's chest, landing a loud smack against his flesh. "I thought he was dead, you imbecile!"

"But, why would you think that?" Cedric blocked her very unladylike attack of slapping hands and backed away. Lilith followed him, enraged all the more when he chuckled at her efforts. "My lady, halt, I beg you. I did not bow down when I took the sword. I know you saw me. I—"

"Bow down?" She stopped hitting, breathing hard. "No one told me you had to bow down—*argh*! These stupid customs should be written down somewhere so they can be read by newcomers like me. How in all the accursed dimensions am I supposed to know these things if I'm not told? If I brought you to my home dimension, do you think you'd get on with no help?"

"Lady makes a good argument," Oskar put forth.

"Why didn't Sorin come himself?" she inquired.

Cedric glanced at Oskar who nodded his permission to answer. "He's been injured."

"Take me to the encampment. Now," she ordered, determined to see Sorin for herself. The fear she felt when she'd thought him dead didn't leave her, and it wouldn't until she could touch him and feel the warmth of his flesh.

"I'm assured he will recover. There is no reason to take you into the marshland in your delicate condition, my lady. Lord Sorin has recovered well in the past. He is strong and a hero. We have great hope—"

"You can tell me everything on the way," Lilith interrupted.

"It will be night before we get—" Cedric again tried to talk her out of her plan.

"Take me to my husband. Now." Lilith turned and strode into the castle to get a blanket for the cart.

"Everything" might have been the wrong command to give. Cedric obeyed, explaining in full detail every gory, horrible second of the attack on the first encampment. By the tone of his voice, it was clear he had no idea how close he was to being thrown up on again.

Lilith's cart ambled toward the newly set up second camp where Starian forces had combined. She'd refused to get on a horse. Thinking it was because of her baby, Cedric agreed to the slower pace of the cart. Lilith did not correct him. What did she care if he thought her pregnant? It's not like she'd started the rumor. And if their misunderstanding made them a tad more accommodating, so be it.

The air became almost stagnant the farther south they traveled, making it hard to breathe. Moss-covered trees lined the wetlands, before spreading into an opened space of shallow waters covered with oddly shaped patches of vegetation. Cedric led her horse right into the marsh, splashing them through the shallow waters before reaching higher ground.

Lilith saw the tops of rectangular tents outlined by firelight, dusk and the large moon, before she heard the gentle murmur of voices coming from the encampment. The smell of burning wood from the bonfires mingled with nature's perfume. Tiny sparks from the flames danced in the evening sky before dying out.

"Do not worry, my lady," Cedric assured her. "The Caniba cannot rise up from the marshes. You will be safe."

The tents, varying in sizes, spread out over the high clearing on an orderly grid to create pathways. The larger tents were in the middle with progressively smaller ones fanning round them. Banners hung from the tent flaps, pinned to the opened entryways. Their brilliant colors stuck out against the light caramel of the canvas.

Lilith searched the gathering crowd for her husband, but didn't see him. Curious eyes stared at her, a few of them familiar, most not. Then, seeing Sorin's crest hanging from a flap, she jumped from the slowing cart and ran for it.

"Sorin?" she called, not stopping to knock. "Are you in here? They said you'd been injured. Cedric wouldn't tell me how badly. What happened? Are you all right?"

Her eyes adjusted to the dim light and no one answered. A pitcher had been placed on a small wooden table. The steady rise and fall of breathing drew her attention to a fur-covered bed. Sorin rested with his hands at his sides, above the fur coverlet.

Someone had bandaged his arms from wrist to shoulder with cloth strips.

"Sorin?" she asked, quieter as she made her way to him. She touched his head, trembling to feel the feverish heat.

"He fought well."

Lilith turned, about to tell whoever spoke that she really hated that saying. Out of respect for Sorin and knowing that "fighting well" was something he took pride in, she stayed quiet. "You're one of his men. Lance, right?"

"Yea, my lady," the redheaded warrior nodded. "I tend to the injured. My family has a gift for it." He crossed to his patient. "His wounds are clean, but his fever won't break. I've given him every herb I know, but now it is up to the gods."

Lilith nodded. After all the emotions that run through her, she now had to face losing him all over again? She wasn't sure she could stand it a second time.

"He's been asking for you. Because he can't travel, I sent for you." Lance touched her shoulder lightly. "Steel yourself. Don't let him see that pity on your face. In his state he might think you are not proud of him. He is a hero, the gods will favor him."

"It's not pity." She rolled her arm away from

Lance's touch. "It's determination. He's not going to die. If he did, I'd die with him and he promised to always protect me. His stubborn pride won't let him go back on his word." She stood next to the bed, looking down at Sorin's pale face. "Do you hear me, my lord? If you don't fight, I'll be right behind you and I'll make your afterlife a living hell. There is no way you're leaving me alone in this forsaken dimension to be claimed by some other man."

Sorin didn't move. Lilith pretended to be brave, hoping that her actions would convince her terrified heart. She reached for a bandage, peeling it back. Long deep gashes created crosshatched patterns over the flesh. What had they done to him?

Lance peered over her shoulder. "I still need to cauterize the wounds on this arm. I did not wish to overtire his body. He's lucky he wore armor. The Caniba tribesmen could not bite through the metal plates."

"How soon until I can take him to Battlewar?" Lilith asked. She couldn't leave him in the marshes. He needed medical care—real medical care—and she knew just the people who had it.

"Why would you wish to move him? If it is supplies you seek, we can send for anything you need."

"I need a handheld medical laser from dimensional plane 187." Lilith redressed the wound, careful not to press too hard. "He appears stable enough if we travel slowly. There is no reason we should risk his life when I can obtain the treatment he needs."

"I cannot allow you to use the Divinity portal." Lance shook his head. "We don't trade off-plane."

She arched a brow. "I'm here, aren't I?"

"Yea, but Lord Ronen spoke to the king and asked him to cease all trades because the women didn't know they were being transported." Lance frowned. "It's been some cause for disappointment amongst the unmarried men."

"Listen to me, Lance. You see a lot of wounds, don't you?"

Lance nodded. "Yea, too many."

"What if I told you I knew of a device that could repair the flesh better than fire and iron? And that these wounds could be healed in two weeks time, possibly faster?"

"This handheld medical laser can do that?"

"Oh, yea, it can do that." She nodded. It took all her willpower not to jump on him and shake him until he came to his senses. Her husband was in pain and she knew how to save him. "I have a cart outside.

If we can load him up and take him to Battlewar, I can get that laser."

"No, I'll go. I cannot let you—"

"Have you been to 187? Have you ever traded with another plane directly?"

Lance frowned, shaking his head in denial.

"I know them. I lived there for two months. I know their customs, their weaknesses. I know how to get that laser." Lilith motioned to Sorin. "Do you wish to see your great war hero suffer like this? He did injure the Sorceress, after all."

Lance nodded. "I'll ready the cart and assemble the men. We'll ride at first light."

"We'll ride now," Lilith corrected.

Lance nodded, hurrying to go.

Lilith sat precariously near Sorin's head. Shaking, she touched his cheek, feeling the heat. "I wish I was as brave as I sounded, but until I am, I'm going to fake it. I know you'd want me to do you proud. I won't dishonor you." She kissed between his eyes, holding her lips against him. "Damn you, my lord, you're not allowed to die on me. Do you hear me, Sorin? I can't live without you. I love you. I need you. Just don't leave me."

"I WANT YOU TO KNOW, my lady, you will be taken care of. We all admire how brave you are and how you honor your husband. You do not have to worry about your babe should—"

Lilith glared up at the man on the horse, cutting him off. After four days, she knew all the men by name. They were pleasant enough for the most part, though she was not in a mood to be social. Every inch of her body ached, she'd barely slept, stress and worry filled her waking moments and Sorin's condition didn't improve. She walked next to Sorin's cart to stretch her legs as they neared Battlewar. Fatigue settled in her shoulders, stiffening her muscles, but she refused to stop. "Do me a favor, Rodrick."

"Anything."

"Spread the word. If any man tries to claim me, ever, he'll wake up a woman." Her meaning wasn't lost. Rodrick gulped and leaned forward on his steed as if to protect his balls. Realizing how mean she sounded, she felt instantly sorry and opened her mouth to apologize, but the knight nudged his horse, riding ahead of her.

Sorin groaned as the cart jerked. Lilith instantly crawled next to him and put her hand gingerly over his heart. The gesture always seemed to calm him. Throughout the journey, he didn't wake up or open his eyes. His fever lifted for a few hours only to come back. She was extremely glad she decided to take him back to Battlewar Castle. If he didn't improve soon, she wasn't sure he ever would.

"We're almost there, my love," she whispered, talking to him softly as she had throughout the journey. Lilith tried to keep the fear out of her voice, even as tears welled in her eyes. It couldn't end like this. She didn't know if he could hear her, but she still tried. "Just a little farther."

To her surprise, he blinked. Glazed eyes found her. Hoarsely, he ground out, "I saw you on the battlefield watching me."

"What do you mean? I wasn't there." Excitement filled her voice. He spoke!

"Don't use the portal."

"I have to. I already told you why." She cupped his whiskered cheek. The scruff of growth scratched her hand. She willed his eyes to clear, to really see her. They didn't.

"Then I forgive you." His eyes closed once more.

"Sorin, for what? You forgive me for what?" She tried to keep him talking, but he passed out. Dismissing his feverish words, she clung to the hope that they weren't too late.

HIS BODY HURT SO BADLY he wasn't sure he still lived. Every inch of him ached—his back from lying down, his wounded arms and legs, his broken heart. Through his dreams he heard Lilith's voice calling to him. Like when he fought on the battlefield, she haunted him.

Not knowing whether he was awake or asleep, he tried to grasp onto the ghostly figure always inches from his tattered hand. She stood, watching him, those big blue eyes tearing into his soul.

"I saw you on the battlefield watching me," he tried to tell her. *I always see you.*

Lilith didn't answer, but he'd heard her words

before. She took him to Battlewar, to the Divinity portal. He knew she wanted to leave him. As much as it was his, this life was not hers.

"Don't use the portal." Sorin hated his weak body. Why didn't he move? *Please, stay with me.*

This time, her ghostly lips parted and he heard her voice. "I have to. I already told you why."

She had told him. Her misery etched itself into his heart. Why didn't the gods just let him die in heroic glory? He was nothing without her. "Then I forgive you."

*If you must go, I will no longer stop you. I forgive you for finding your happiness, lady wife, and for taking my heart. But, please, I beg you to choose me. Stay. Forever. All I am is yours. I am undone by you. You have conquered me.*

LILITH STARED AT THE DIALS, her hand shaking. No one would know if she dialed home until it was too late. Someone at Divinity could bring a medical laser back. They had plenty of them in the store room. She could leave Staria and find justice for what had been done to her and the others.

She could leave. Forever.

"If my lady hesitates, I will go in her place. Instruct me." Rodrick placed a hand on her shoulder. His boyish crush was harmless enough, and she knew it was because he met very few women out on the battlefield. She understood why the Starians bartered for brides, but that didn't make it right, at least not when the women had been kidnapped.

"No. There's no time." She turned a couple of the dials. Dimensional plane 187's coordinates were memorized by all Divinity employees in case of an emergency. The doctors on the other side would help her with little question, so long as she gave them the clearance codes and a little incentive. "Did you bring it?"

"Here," Rodrick handed her a vial. Hopefully it would be enough.

"But the child..."

"Rodrick, there is no child," Lilith answered, wondering why it hurt so much to say the words out loud. She'd let everyone believe she was pregnant, never once correcting their assumption. "It was only a rumor. No one thought to ask me if it were true."

She thought of Sorin and her decision was simple. She couldn't go. Not yet. He may never come to love her, but his presence would be enough. She might never adjust, she might grow bored and bitter, but right now, she knew what must be done.

"Stay back from the light!" Lilith ordered. She didn't hesitate again as she set the dials. Then, pushing a button, she turned to the domed arch over the innocuous-looking center platform. The blue light shifted to pale green as she walked toward the portal. The closer she got, the more the light lured her in.

Suddenly, the strong gravitational field pulled her off her feet, hurling her toward the back of the platform. Defensively, she curled her arms over her head and closed her eyes tight, braced for impact. She clenched the vial tight, careful not to let go. The concentrated light burned and every cell in her body felt heavy. She couldn't move as her head hit the back wall. But what should have been a hard crash was only a moderate brush across her scalp.

No matter how many times she went through, she would never get used to the sensation of being pulled apart at a molecular level. Like riding on a bad carnival ride, she kept still and stiff and waited for the second it would be over. The pull stopped and her body dropped with a hard thud on a metal platform.

"Ugh," she moaned, coughing as her body

adjusted to the abrupt freedom. The blue light shone from above in a less primitive version of the Starian portal. A loud alarm blared overhead, buzzing annoyingly. The smell of metal and 187's air-filtering sterilizer wafted over her.

"Sterilization commencing. Please stand and move away from the platform."

Lilith trembled weakly, but pushed to her feet to obey the male, automated voice. If she didn't let them sweep her for other dimensional parasites and viruses, they'd stick her in quarantine for a year. A shield came down, blocking the platform from the scan as a series of lights flashed over her.

"Sterilization complete. Please state your clearance code."

"Lilith Grian. Divinity Corporation Analyst. Employee number 54367D."

"Accepted. Please move to the orange door."

The door was actually metallic gray with a series of numbers and letters written in orange across the front. It opened automatically and she passed through. It might have been awhile, but she remembered the layout well enough. Every facility on 187 had the same architectural design. The citizens were obsessed with immortality, and each worked for the central hospital government in some capacity.

"Sans Grian," Dr. Lu greeted. His long blue coat with red trim was standard issue for the facility, as was his shortly cropped hair, his perfectly groomed eyebrows and his manicured nails. "Welcome back to our facility." He looked at an orange electronic clipboard and frowned. "Your scans show no injury or illness and you're not due for a physical. I do see low levels of homytobin and plytomikin. Not threatening to life, but known to cause fatigue." He reached into his pocket and took out a syringe. Like everything else it was electronic. He pressed the tip to the clipboard, waited for a beep and then leaned forward to press it to her bare neck. "That boost should take care of the deficiency. Good day, Sans Grian. I will send a copy of your record to Divinity Corporation Headquarters."

She wasn't surprised by the dismissal. If anything, 187 was efficient. "Wait, Dr. Lu. I'm not here for me. I'm here to barter for a handheld unit."

He turned, again looking to his clipboard. "Divinity has several in working order. I don't see why—"

"I have trade." She lifted the vial. "Blue mineral water from an underground spring. It has very unique properties. I doubt Divinity's shown it to you yet. They'll want to wait until they need a big favor."

His eyes lit with interest as he looked at it. "What kind of properties?"

"Feel it for yourself." She tossed it at him. He dropped his clipboard, not even seeming to notice as he studied the vial. "It stays warm, even when not exposed to a heat source. Just think of the possibilities. Deaths by freezing will be eliminated. Mountain climbers, deep sea divers, all your medical expedition teams can go longer and farther."

"Where...?"

"I'm not sure of the dimensions coordinates, but if you give me a handheld and reverse the portal I just came from, it's all yours." She smiled, knowing she had him. Scientists couldn't resist such temptations.

"I will have to get the proper clearance." Dr. Lu didn't take his eyes from the mineral water.

"I'll need you to hurry. A friend of mine doesn't have much time." She thought of Sorin in so much pain. His condition seemed steady, but she couldn't help the urge to hurry. Before, traveling to a new dimension, even one she'd been to before, would have thrilled her. Now, she found herself annoyed by the hum of the overhead lights and the sterile smell of air.

He reached for his clipboard, refusing to let go of

the new find. Pushing the clipboard's surface a couple times, he lifted it up and began to speak. Lilith watched in silence as he transmitted his image to other doctors in the facility, telling them of her arrival and of her proposal. Finishing, he said, "I call for a vote."

*Just a few more seconds... Come on, hurry.*

Lilith tapped her foot, eager to leave but understanding their protocol in such matters. By the light in Dr. Lu's eyes, the trade would be a done deal. The sound of footfalls echoed along the hall, and she automatically moved to the side to let a couple of the doctors pass.

"Denied," an authoritative voice answered through the clipboard. "Please escort Sans Grian to Security Observation Five. She is to be detained in accordance with treaty law..."

"What?" Lilith screamed, ready to bolt. The two doctors she'd moved over for had stopped. They grabbed her arms. Dr. Lu held the vial in his palm as he led the way to the security wing. Kicking her feet, she jerked violently. "What are you doing? I came for a simple, peaceful trade. Stop at once!"

They didn't listen and they didn't let go.

"Please, I have to get back. Please..."

WARM, soft hands touched him, gliding over every inch of Sorin's flesh. He knew those hands, the way they dipped and explored every curve as if mesmerized by his form. Every part of him felt on fire, burning in agony as if he'd been set on fire.

*Lower.*

His cock ached, so hard and tortured. He couldn't move his limbs to take it. In fact, his body didn't seem to work at all, except for the hard mass surging painfully between his thighs. He couldn't move, couldn't look to see Lilith's face. Oh, how he wanted to look at her! It was one of his great pleasures to watch her move.

*By all the gods, lower.*

After what seemed to be an eternity, she finally complied, running a tormenting trail over his stomach and hips. Every part of him tensed. What would it be? Her mouth? Her hand? The sweet creamy heat of her sex? Sorin didn't care, so long as she released the pain her nearness caused.

*Finish me. Oh, blessed night, finish me.*

Random images filtered through his mind, thoughts of her bent over on her bed as he took her from behind, of her pressed against the bumpy stone wall in the brewery cellar, of how she'd sucked his cock after knife-throwing practice in a small alcove behind the castle.

Mmm, those lips, soft pink disconcerting lips. How he'd liked the way her hair appeared to radiate sunlight even in the shadows. Her breasts bobbed, only giving him a teasing peek through the scarf. At first he wasn't sure, but now he liked that she hid her charms from others. They were his. She was his.

Sorin shifted his hips at the memory, finally breaking free of the paralysis. He remembered clearly how it looked to watch his cock slide in and out of her mouth, going in dry only to come out glistening and wet. Lilith seemed to enjoy it as well. She moaned into him, sucking as if she'd drain the essence from him and leave him for dead. Her hand rolled his balls and she gripped his hip tight. Sorin groaned. The memory so vivid he felt the graze of her teeth, the press of her lips, the lick of her tongue.

*Yea, Lilith, finish me. Oh, by the gods, finish me. I need you to...*

Sorin tensed, his hips jerking so hard it shook his entire body. Moisture flooded his stomach and he jolted awake, glancing down to see wet cum gleaming on his flesh. Dazed from release, he blinked heavily and looked around. His head felt light and dampened by a strange, cool sweat.

"Lilith?" The word came out in a stranger's voice, croaking and hoarse. He cleared his throat, coughing before trying again. "My lady?" The sound was little better.

"My lord? Are you awake?"

Sorin frowned, turning his head to the doorway. This wasn't his chamber—not the tent or the Black Tower. Seeing Sera, he deduced he was at Battlewar Castle. He must have been in common quarters above the main hall.

"How...?" He frowned, feeling a burning along his arms. He looked at the bandages, noticing the pain in them for the first time upon waking.

"Shh." Sera rushed in and grabbed his coverlet, pulling the fur over his naked body. He barely registered the fact that the evidence of his desire for his wife lay across his stomach. The servant touched his head. "You were wounded at battle, my lord, but you did honor to your family name. You wounded the Sorceress, proving she is mortal. All of Staria sings your praises."

"Where...?" His muscles ached and his head pounded violently from the effort to sit up.

Sera pushed him down. "No, my lord, do not.

Lance said we should not move you after so hard a journey."

"Why am I here? Why not leave me at the camp?" He frowned. This time he knocked Sera's hand aside when she tried to hold him down.

The servant refused to answer as she stood to retrieve a pitcher from the table. Pouring him a goblet of water, she brought it back to him. "I've been by your side, tending you, my lord. You have not been the easiest of patients. You need to drink and eat more."

"Why have you tended me? Where is...?" He stopped mid-drink and lowered the goblet before it touched his lips. "Where is my wife?"

"My lord, you shouldn't upset yourself. Lance said—"

"I do not care what Lance said, Sera," Sorin yelled. "Where is my wife?"

"She's not here, my lord." The servant eyed him fearfully as she backed toward the door.

"What do you mean she's not here?" Sorin gripped the goblet. The soreness of his throat and dryness of his mouth forced him to drink its contents. Even so, he didn't take his deadly eyes off Sera.

"She left, my lord."

"Left?" Fear gripped him. *No.* "Where?"

He knew the answer before she said it. "Through the portal. Please, my lord, do not get up. You must rest."

"When?"

"Five days ago. The same day you arrived here." At his dangerous look, she rushed on to explain. "She said she was going to get a medical device to cure you and would be right back. Rodrick took responsibility for her and brought her to the portal. He waited for her return, but when it became clear she would not he had himself locked in the dungeon to await your punishment for losing her. I'm sorry, my lord, but she has—"

Sorin yelled, throwing the goblet at the wall. The metal clanged on the blue-grey stone, but the loud noise did not satisfy him. Sera yelped, jumping in alarm as she ran for the door. Enraged, he tried to get out of bed, making it to his feet. The second he stood, his world spun in fast circles around him, and he felt himself falling backward as darkness consumed his mind.

THE ONLY ADVANTAGE to being held against her will by a dimension obsessed with health was she'd never felt physically better in her life. They forced her to exercise for a precisely calculated amount of time. They took her "not optimal for total health" clothing to be destroyed, replacing the Starian outfit with a pair of slacks and loose long shirt in the red and blue facility colors. Every meal, though bland, was perfectly balanced with her body's dietary needs for the day. And whenever her stomach started to churn with stress and worry, someone came to give her a shot in the neck to take the symptoms away. But no shot in all the worlds could end how she felt about Sorin.

Did he worsen? Had he awakened? Did he know she'd left? She could only imagine what everyone thought when she didn't return.

"Sans Grian," the automated voice said, "your lidic levels are rising again. A medic has been dispatched..."

"...to blah blah blah blah blah," she mocked loudly, not stopping her restless pacing around the small room. White walls and metal accoutrements surrounded her—precise, clean and irritatingly lacking in craftsmanship. She missed her thick cushiony bed and the carved detail of her furniture. She missed banners and towering castles. She missed her warrior husband. "If you really want to cure me, robot, send me home."

The automated voice didn't answer.

The door slid open and Lilith didn't bother looking to see who'd come to shoot her in the neck this time. She turned on her heels, walking away from the door.

*Sorin, please be all right. I'm sorry I couldn't get the handheld to you. I tried to escape. I tried to get back to you. I—*

"Lilith, how surprising to see you here."

Lilith stiffened. She knew that voice. "Director Carretta?"

"I admit to being a little stunned when the Medical Supreme contacted us as to your detainment, especially when you had no apparent injuries and thus no reason to seek this dimension," the director answered. "I rather like to think there was a certain man friend you wanted to look up, but your profile doesn't sustain the theory."

"I didn't realize I needed to be detained." Lilith slowly turned, facing the woman.

Samanta Carretta smiled politely, but the look couldn't be trusted. The mission director always wore that expression. Slim and gorgeous, with smooth dark skin and short black hair, Carretta could turn any man's head. However, that gorgeous innocence was her most dangerous weapon. Carretta could kill a man twice her size in under three moves, before he even realized she planned to attack.

"Of course we put a detainment bulletin out for you. What did you think would happen when you disappeared with a sacred artifact from 228?" Carretta clicked her tongue, coming all the way into the room. The door slid shut behind her. "Very naughty, Miss Grian. I have to admit, we never suspected you for a thief. Had we known your predilection, we'd have put your talents to better use instead of having you waste away doing cultural analyses."

"I didn't take the book," Lilith defended.

"Then how do you explain the traces of the text found in your crate. Your thumbprint was on the seal."

"It's a mistake," Lilith said, defensively holding up her hands. "I packed that crate myself. I didn't steal any sacred book. I only took the copies they said I could have for the Divinity archive. When I got back, I found the book stuffed in the bottom. The magistrate on 228 showed me the book when I took a tour of their archives. They had it locked up. There is no way I'd take it on accident."

"Hm," Carretta hummed thoughtfully. She reached into her pocket and pulled out a black box and fingered it gingerly. "So you admit you took it on purpose. Who did you sell it to?"

"I didn't take it." Lilith backed away from the box. Fear gripped her. The director didn't believe her. "When I discovered what had happened, I followed protocol. I turned the item over to Director Tomes. He sent me home and said I'd be contacted after an investigation to give my report of the events. The next thing I know I'd been transported to an uncharted dimension filled with barbarians."

"Director Tomes? That's an interesting story, Miss Grian, but there's no need for you to explain. I think we'll have our answers soon enough." Carretta tapped the top and long thin blades shot out of both sides. Lilith flinched, her back hitting the wall. The director's smile stayed perfectly intact. "Don't look so worried. Over half the people we use this on survive without brain damage."

## 15

"SHOW ME WHAT SHE DID," Sorin ordered, shoving the unresisting Rodrick at the control panel. It took two days for him to gather enough strength to walk down the stairs and, as sure as battles were bloody, he was not going to stop now. The castle didn't stir at such a late hour, and he'd gotten no resistance from the sleeping guard who watched over Rodrick.

"My lord, your wounds," Rodrick pleaded. "I know what you plan. The king ordered that none should go through the portal, but if you insist on following her, let me go in your stead."

Sorin knew the man's fear. It was an emotion they all shared. None of them liked the idea of traveling to different worlds, their bodies sucked into nothingness and disappearing into the unknown.

The king had ordered they take their dealing with Divinity slowly and cautiously. Besides, none of them knew how to navigate the system. Divinity warned them that if they were to try, they might end up in the middle of some dark ocean a thousand feet down or worse.

"She is my wife. I will go." Sorin gave him another shove. His limbs hurt but he'd bound them tightly. "Show me."

"The dials have not been moved." Rodrick flattened his hands to motion over the controls. "All she did was press this button and then walked there." He pointed to the platform Divinity built them. "It carried her off her feet and swallowed her into the light."

Sorin limped to the platform and stood in the center. He'd seen others leave and knew what he had to do. "If I do not return, tell Ronen the family honor rests with him. Tell him I do what duty demands I do."

Rodrick nodded. "Fight well, my lord."

Sorin touched the sword at his waist. It wasn't his blade, but the weapon would work just as well. Inside he was bound into knots, knowing he might never see his homeland again. He got a sense of what Lilith must have felt, waking up in his world with no idea of how she got there. Part of him believed it to be the will of the gods. Why else would they bring her to him? The rest of him didn't know what to believe.

"Press it." The hard command sounded confident and brave, nothing like what he felt inside. Who knew what kind of place he'd find on the other end of this thing?

Rodrick pushed the button and the light began to change. Sorin stood at the ready, gripping the hilt of the sword. He ignored the weakness of his body as his limbs pulled toward the ground. The brightening light burned into his eyes, forcing them to close.

He tensed. The force against his body increased, pulling at his wounds until it felt as if they ripped open beneath the bandages. Sorin suppressed a scream of agony. Then it was over. The pain lessened and he stood, breathing heavily, covered in sweat and shaking like he'd just run from Battlewar to the borderlands.

Opening his eyes, he steeled his nerves. The strange silver box of a chamber appeared to be carved into metal. His nose wrinkled as he tasted the sickeningly sweet air. Stumbling forward, he tried to get his bearings. Metal room. Three doors painted with colored numbers. Portal. Loud buzzing. He flinched, cupping his ears.

"Sterilization commencing. Please remain away from the platform."

Sorin jolted, spinning in circles with his sword raised, as he looked for the owner of the docile male voice. A wall slid down from the ceiling, blocking the portal. Sorin charged it, banging his fist to the metal. The action jolted his arm, but he barely noticed. Lights began to flash all around him, disorienting him with their random pattern.

"Sterilization complete. Multiple unclosed injuries and fluid detected. Please state your clearance code."

"I'm here for my wife," Sorin yelled, menacingly. "Bring her to me."

"Please repeat, clearance code not accepted."

"I am Lord Sorin of Firewall and I demand you bring me my wife!" He lifted his sword, searching for the origin of the voice.

"Unauthorized entry detected." The buzzing grew to an awful earsplitting pitch, pulsing rhythmically. The ceiling opened and an oblong sphere attached to a skinny pole lowered. "Containment orders commencing."

"Give me my wife!" Sorin glared at the speaking sphere as it tried to blind him with a flash. He growled, swinging at with his sword. The weapon sliced through the pole, killing the talking orb with a giant, showering spark.

He rushed the door with green writing. Not finding a handle, he thrust his sword along the edge to open it. Within he found an open area with several tiny beds spread out before him. Each bed held a sleeping person while people in blue and red uniforms walked around them. At the sound of the crashing door, eyes widened in panic as several faces turned to him.

*What in all the burning forests is this place?*

A nearby woman screamed, nearly tripping over a bed to get away from him. When several of the males charged forward, Sorin slammed the door and ran to open the orange one. He kicked the dead sphere out of his way so he could thrust his sword along the edge.

"Unauthorized entry orange hall. Please cease your progress. Sealing for detainment." The voice was back.

Sorin searched the metal corridor for the sphere, expecting it to be on the floor, rolling after him. His heart beat heavily in his chest. This was nothing like he'd imagined. How could this world be a version of his? He stumbled on the smoothed floor, tripping through the endless tunnel, unable to see aught by walls that wound around forever.

*Lilith, where are you?*

Was this her world? No wonder she felt so out of place in his.

"Lilith!" he yelled, quickening his pace. "Bring me Lilith!"

"Hmm, interesting." Director Carretta stared at the medical clipboard she held. Lilith heard and saw everything, but she couldn't react. The truth box had been fastened to her head. It projected her memories in painful reality as a holographic image and forced the truth from her mouth. She'd heard the devices hurt, but nothing could prepare her for the slow, agonizing sensation of her brain being stabbed and probed without numbing. "It seems we have a visitor."

Lilith tried to moan, but only a trickle of drool made its way over her chin. Her body stayed slumped against the wall. Internally connected to the machine on her head, she knew exactly which images it pried from her thoughts. A picture of Director Tomes appeared.

"No, not Tomes. I've already contacted head-quarters about him. It seems you've been telling the truth." Carretta knelt on the floor and held up her clipboard in front of Lilith's face. "Recognize this man?"

Sorin!

He charged though the halls, screaming like a crazed warrior and brandishing a sword. Her heart filled with longing and surprise. What was he doing on 18? How? Why? Thoughts of him were forced from her mind and a rush of images flashed overhead. Carretta stood up in surprise, her eyes rounding as she watched incredibly intimate memories.

"Stop there," Carretta commanded. The memory of holding down Sorin's arms as she rode him came to the forefront of her thoughts. Firelight illuminated his thick muscles and shone on her bouncing breasts. The director's breathing deepened and she slammed the clipboard face down, shutting it off. "I had no idea you were so..."

Lilith tried to think of something else, but she couldn't. The memory aroused her, as real as if she still lived it. Her pussy moistened and she wanted to feel the thick length of her husband conquering her.

Carretta leaned closer, staring above Lilith's head to the projection. Whispering, she ordered, "Show me his cock." The scene changed to one of Lilith about to take him into her mouth, freezing like a snapshot. Carretta licked her lips. "He's huge. I'll bet he knows how to take a woman."

"Yes," Lilith answered, unable to control it.

Carretta's hand brushed her thigh and she leaned into Lilith's ear. "Show me. I want to watch him come."

The scene played in all its realistic detail. Lilith tasted his flesh, felt the probe of his cock as it pushed past her teeth.

Carretta walked out of her eye line. "I'll bet he tastes good."

"Yes," Lilith answered. "Unlike anything you've ever savored."

"Will you let me taste him?" Carretta's breathing had become ragged and harsh. "I don't care if you watch. I just want that cock in my mouth."

"You touch him and I'll rip out your heart, you fucking cunt bitch," Lilith threatened, though she was in no position to follow through with it.

"Well, at least I know you're not lying," Carretta chuckled. "I don't blame you. I'd be possessive too."

Sorin's body tensed in the memory, becoming tight as he jerked his release into her mouth. She tasted his cum. Carretta moaned softly, making a strange noise.

After a moment, the woman asked, "Are all these Starians like that? When you said primitive, I didn't think to look at them. I thought cavemen, or dirty barbaric..." A scene of the main hall, of the first time Lilith had walked into the crowd of lusty knights, formed.

"Yes, they are all well formed."

"Tell me about them," she ordered.

"They lack inhibitions and women," Lilith began, before going into a detailed analysis of Starian culture. By the time she'd finished, Carretta was sitting in front of her with sparkling eyes.

"I must have one for my collection," she said. "Tell me, do you want to go back there?"

"Yes, with all my heart."

"Even though they don't fall in love?"

The fact hurt, but she answered, "Yes. I love him."

"Here's where we stand, Miss Grian. Director Tomes will be arrested and tried for the theft of the sacred text. I'm supposed to bring you back to head-quarters for reassignment," Carretta scratched her manicured nails against her palm. "But clearly there's some explaining to be done to the Starian government, and we're going to need someone to mediate this mess he made. I didn't know about Tomes' trade agreement. Kidnapped women are bad business, but we can't very well go back on a deal, can we? I swear, for a smart man, Tomes is an idiot. If he needed volunteers all he had to do was market the product. Plenty of women would sign on to be the wife of such virile specimens."

Lilith couldn't move or speak.

"Besides, that blue water you brought does show potential. The doctors thought the vial was our stolen artifact and they're salivating to get their hands on it. There's some trade to be done here." Carretta glanced at the hall filled with warriors. "I also have a personal interest in assuring trades continue. Someone's going to have to go to Staria as an ambassador and such trips do have their perks." Her catlike smile gave full meaning to the perks she planned on partaking in. "I'll make you a deal. I'll send you back with lover boy and instate you as our official liaison with the Starian people. You'll integrate yourself into their customs, live there, become an expert in Starian politics and in return we'll continue the trade—only this time with willing women. I'll also expect there to be a plethora of willing men of a certain stamina to choose from when I arrive. I have appetites, but I'm not a monster. I like my participants enthusiastic."

"Yes," Lilith agreed. She highly doubted finding lonely men eager for a romp would be hard. "Deal."

"Oh, but there's one last thing. You are never, ever, not under pain of torture, allowed to tell the folks at headquarters about the nature of my visits. Who I plan to fuck or how many at one time is none of their business. You keep my secret and I'll make sure your dimension is listed as an uninteresting trade plane and buried in a back file."

"Deal," Lilith repeated. Her heart began to race.

"Let's get this off you." Carretta tapped the box once. The thin blades retracted. "I believe there's a crazed maniac on the loose screaming your name, and the good doctors are frantic that he needs medical attention. Apparently, he's dripping blood all over their halls." She picked up her clipboard, the motion turning it back on. "The man looks fine to me."

As soon as the box released control, Lilith screamed, gripping her head.

Carretta flinched at the sound. "Yeah, sorry about the inconvenience, but we had to know the truth. Dimensional harmony is a delicate thing."

*Lilith!*

Her scream echoed all around him and Sorin pressed on through the endless maze of halls. They didn't go anywhere, just looped around. His drops of blood marked his fruitless path. He couldn't find a door and, except for the occasionally annoying male voice announcing a "lock down", he didn't hear anything.

Until now.

Lilith's screams propelled him on. He grabbed his thigh, pressing into a bite wound. Sweat beaded his brow at the effort it took to move. His strength depleted fast and he hadn't even fought. But he couldn't stop. Not now. Lilith needed him.

"Lilith?" he yelled, the tip of his sword dragging behind him.

He shouldn't be so weak. Even when he'd been gouged in the stomach he'd managed better than this. He blinked heavily. The corridor wall slid up and the screams became louder. Just a few more steps.

Sorin wavered on his feet as he stumbled to the door. The sword became heavy and dropped with a loud clang. Lilith writhed on the floor, clutching her face as a black creature with silver legs attacked her head. Another woman stood next to her, arms crossed and expression calm.

Sorin fell to his knees in the doorway. Why couldn't he stand? His vision swam, causing Lilith's form to dance before him. He dropped to the floor, rolling onto his back.

"Sorin," Lilith called his name, but he couldn't reach her.

The dark-haired woman stepped to him, peering down. "Perhaps the Medical Supreme should reconsider the security dosage in his hallways. You breathed in enough sleeping dust to take down twelve normal men. But then, you're not a normal man, are you?" She knelt beside his prone body and gave a secretive laugh. "I think I'm going to like this arrangement we have with your dimension, Lord Sorin. Yes, indeed."

LILITH STRETCHED her neck as she turned on her side. Sorin lay on the cot next to her. It took a little convincing on Carretta's part, but the woman knew how to manipulate, and she soon had Sorin under the best medical treatment in all the dimensions. Even in her irritation over being put through the truth box hell, Lilith couldn't help but be grateful for the help. How could she hate Carretta when with each passing second Sorin's color darkened to a healthy glow?

He was there in front of her. She nearly squealed with excitement. In her darkest times, she feared she'd never see him again, feared his death.

The doctors had made some advances since Lilith visited last. One painted muscle tissue into Sorin's wounds, healing them from within before another sprayed skin regenerate. Almost visibly the gashes healed and the old scars lessened. Several medical students were even brought by to witness the progress. It was rare they had such a broken specimen to work with.

Lilith had to hide her amusement when one of the doctors, a short, slender man, said with obvious disdain, "Look at the primitive display of muscular tissue due to excessive exercise and improper diet." The female students all glanced at each other, staring at the "primitive display" of Sorin on the bed, but obviously not as disgusted by the look of him as the instructor.

*Let them stare,* she thought. *They can't have him. He's all mine.*

"Can we examine the specimen more closely?" a

woman asked, leaning over to pull at Sorin's covers. Her eyes were unmistakably on his cock.

"Back off, Red," Lilith warned, stiffening, "or your classmates will learn about limb reattachment."

The woman yelped and ran. The other students trailed behind her at a slower pace. Lilith smiled victoriously.

"Scan," a medic said, coming to the bed with a handheld. Lilith didn't move as the man worked. He pressed his syringe to the unit before leaning over to give Lilith whatever medicine she required. The tension in her head lessened.

"I am glad to see you have a fighting spirit."

"Sorin?" Lilith's eyes rounded and she pushed up. He didn't look at her, but that was definitely his voice.

"No, do not move. I hear three others on the far side of the room. As soon as they're gone, we're getting out of here." He definitely spoke, but his lips barely moved, and his chest rose and fell in even breath.

"But—"

"I won't let them hurt you anymore," he swore. His eyes opened a sliver so he could look at her. "I won't fail you."

"Sorin, I'm fine. They didn't hurt me. Well, it

hurt, but it was just a mind probe. I had to clear my name." There was so much she needed to explain, but the sound of his voice flustered her and she couldn't think of all she wanted to say to him.

"Then this is your home."

"No, it's not. It's 187, a medical dimension."

"You were not coming back to me." He frowned, his eyes opening further. Lilith slid off the bed and went to sit next to him. He gave up the pretense of sleep and looked at her in confusion.

"I tried," she whispered, not wanting the doctors to overhear. "I came here to get medicine to help you heal. Your wounds were so bad and Lance said you'd recover, but I saw the uncertainty in him. Everyone kept telling me to trust in the gods, they'd reward a hero, and maybe they did. You're here and you're healed. But before, you were in so much pain and your fever wouldn't break. Then you started mumbling incoherent thoughts. I had to come."

His frown deepened.

"I did plan on returning to help you, but Divinity had a bulletin out on me and my arrival set off the security systems. They wouldn't let me leave until Director Carretta cleared me of all charges. It seems I was sent to your world to cover up a theft." She touched his face. "What are you doing here? Why did you jump into a portal? You had no way of knowing what awaited you on the other side or if you'd even make it back."

"I came for you," he stated, his expression softening. "I knew you wanted to leave my world, but I had to check on you. You are my wife. I would jump through a million portals to look for you."

"Sorin, I—"

"No, do not say it. Let me speak." He pushed up. The covers dropped around his waist, revealing a smooth, naked chest. She couldn't resist touching him, as she ran her hand down the center of his chest to rest between his pectorals. His warmth worked its way into her fingertips, spreading awareness down her arm. "I understand that coming to me was not of your choice, but I believe it happened for a reason. If you cannot stay in my world, then let me stay in yours. I will learn your ways. I will live within these unnatural walls and breathe this sweet air, if it pleases you to have me do so."

"What about your home? Your family?"

"Ronen will carry on the family name," he stated. Cupping her face, he said, "You bewitched me from the moment I first saw you. I swore after Bianka that I would never take another wife but one look and I was yours. In battle, I could not concentrate for fear you would not be there when I came home. I cannot survive without you, my lady wife. When Sera said you went through the portal, I died inside. So I beg you, go seek your happiness in whatever world you choose, only take me with you."

Lilith gasped and a hot tear rolled over her cheek, hitting his hand. "I want to go home."

"Then we'll go home," he assured her, leaning in to press his lips to hers. "What is this world of yours like?"

She gave a teary laugh. "It's filled with stubborn men with strange customs and noble battles. There are castles made of stone and torchlight and were clearly named by men for no woman would ever name a home after a weapon. The air smells of earth and flowers. The servants are annoying, but it's all worth it at the end of the day because I have you."

"You would choose a life with me?" He looked around the metal room.

"There is no choice, Sorin. I love you." She ran her hands into his hair, thoroughly kissing him. His tongue slid into her mouth, deep and sure. Lilith shivered, forgetting everything but his touch.

"You were telling the truth. They are uninhibited." Carretta chuckled from the end of the bed.

"Please, don't stop on my account. I don't mind taking in a good show now and again."

Sorin stiffened, pulling Lilith into his protective embrace. She put her hands on her husband's chest and pushed gently so she could look at him. "Everything's fine. I'll explain it to you once we're back home."

"I see you're healed, Lord Sorin." Carretta nodded in satisfaction. "Unfortunately though, they don't carry shirts in your size and they burned your clothes—a strange custom here. Fear of parasites and natural fibers, you understand. You'll have to wear the blanket home."

Sorin looked at his arms, his eyes rounding as if he'd noticed them for the first time. "How long did I sleep?"

"A few hours," Lilith said. "This is why I wanted a handheld. Think of the lives we can save with it."

"Ah, speaking of..." Carretta reached down to pick up a canvas bag. "As part of the mineral water trade agreement I just signed, Staria is presented with its own medical unit with complete accessories and enough injectible meds to cure ten thousand big beefy warriors for hundreds of years. Instruction manual and your very own Divinity translation guide included."

"You negotiated a hand-held for Staria?" Lilith asked in surprise, reaching to take the offering.

"Don't tell management." Carretta winked. "Besides, we can't have them getting sick. Be sure they get the booster pack. Hurry up. I'm expected back at headquarters tomorrow morning."

"We need to talk about a few things first," Lilith said. "Not only must the females you bring be willing, but they will come awake and aware, with full health screens and documentation."

"Yes, yes." Carretta waved her hand in dismissal. "Of course, all that."

"And I want my belongings delivered, a data unit with a copy of the recipe database in a language readable by the castle's kitchen staff. I want a—"

"Write it all down," the director interrupted. "I'm sure everything you want can be met. Now, about my wants... Let's go. I believe you promised to introduce me to unattached men."

"Is she a..." Sorin studied Carretta as she sauntered away, "camp follower?"

Lilith snorted with laughter, covering her mouth. "She's one of the top people at Divinity. I've only talked to her a handful of times."

"Come here." Sorin made a small noise in the

back of his throat as he leaned in to kiss her. "I wish to finish what we began."

"Sorin!" Lilith said under her breath, blushing profusely. "We can't do that here."

He grinned. "I meant the talking, but I assure you I feel well enough for the other."

Lilith glanced to where the redheaded student stared at them from across the room. Hefting the canvas bag onto her shoulder, she said, "Let's go home, my lord husband. We have the rest of our lives to talk."

"You're sure this will make you happy?"

"You will make me happy." She slugged his arm lightly. "At least you better."

He grinned, a completely saucy look filled with promise. Standing from the bed, he pulled the covers with him, holding them at his waist. Lilith walked beside him toward the portal.

She moaned softly, twining her fingers around his muscular arm. "I won't feel right until I'm safely tucked away in our bed."

"Our bed?" He lifted a brow.

"Yep, I decided you're never leaving my side, my lord." She smiled happily, leaning her head next to him.

"Then I feel duty bound to tell you, my lady." He

untangled himself from her hold and slid his hands over her shoulders. They made their way through the hall, both eager to get to their dimension. "You do snore. Loudly."

Lilith gasped, hitting him in mock affront. "You will pay for your insults."

"Warriors are not frightened by torture." He paused as they reached the orange door. The lock had been scraped and broken. Sorin chuckled at his handiwork, the sound filled with masculine warrior pride.

"About time. I've set the coordinates," Carretta stated. "I'll let you go through first. I'd hate to cause alarm arriving unannounced."

Lilith led Sorin to the platform. Her heart fluttered inside her chest when she looked into his eyes. "I meant it when I said I love you. I know you don't put much faith in the emotion, but everything I am belongs to you."

"You are my heart, Lilith." He brought her hand and pressed it to his chest. "I am nothing without you. If that is not love, then I do not understand the meaning."

She lifted up on her toes to kiss him, but a brilliant red light washed over them, pulling them through the portal.

## 16

"Lord Sorin!" Rodrick shouted in excitement.

Lilith gasped as she materialized next to her husband. They both stumbled apart as gravity released them from its clutches.

"Lady Lilith! Blessed night, you made it!" Rodrick continued.

The couple grinned. Lilith pulled Sorin out of the way before Carretta came through and landed on their heads.

"And you're healed!" Rodrick hurried forward, lifting Sorin's arm to examine it in amazement, as if he looked at a god himself. Suddenly, he snickered, "And soft as a newborn's backside."

Sorin frowned, looking down as if seeing his body for the first time. He grabbed his stomach, dropping the covers from his waist. "They took my scars." Lifting his arm, he shouted in disbelief, "My mark of manhood. Those accursed gnomes took my mark."

"Ah," Lilith mouthed in surprise. Out of all the things to get upset over, she hadn't expected that.

"Now it looks as if I've never seen a battle!" Sorin proceeded to examine his perfectly smooth skin for old war wounds. He touched his thigh. "The lance Ronen hit me with as a child. It's gone." Sorin began to charge the platform, completely naked. "We're going back and demanding they return—"

"Sorin." Lilith hurried after him, pulling him back. The platform flashed and Carretta appeared, wobbling on her feet. She'd mussed up her hair and had put on makeup before coming through.

"Mm, I like it, very dungeonesque." Carretta's eyes found Rodrick. "Please tell me you're not married."

"Rodrick, consider her your punishment for losing my wife," Sorin muttered.

"Oh, punishment, I like that." Carretta batted her lashes, walking around the stunned Rodrick like he was a piece of meat and she was the butcher. The poor knight didn't stand a chance. His round eyes stared at her and his breathing deepened. Lilith was pretty sure his boyish crush on her was over the second Carretta grabbed him by the front of his tunic and pulled. "Come on, you naughty boy. Show me where you keep the prisoners."

"Wow, around headquarters I had no idea she was like that," Lilith whispered. "You do realize what you just ordered Rodrick to do, don't you?"

"He can handle himself in battle, he can handle that witch." Sorin grunted. "She will make him a man."

"Rodrick's a virgin?" Lilith really felt sorry for the guy. When she turned back to her husband, he had started examining himself again. Licking her lips, she let herself enjoy the sight of his naked body cast in blue light. She ran her hand over his firm ass, raking it with her nails. "You know, if you're really upset about how the doctors healed you..."

Sorin's head snapped up as she gripped his butt cheek hard. "Yea?"

"I can think of a few ways to mar that pretty flesh of yours that doesn't include bloody battlefields." Lilith nipped at his back. She'd never really hurt him, but it was fun to play. Now that she knew his true feelings, every last hesitation flittered away. She was his, completely and forever. Sliding her hand around, she pressed to his back and grabbed his cock. "And when we're done, you won't need a tattoo to remind you that you are a man."

Sorin growled, spinning on his heels to face her. He caught her up easily, tossing her over his shoulder. The canvas bag remained on the floor, forgotten.

"Sorin, wait, you're naked! The hall..." Lilith kicked her feet, laughing as he hurried to the stairs. He didn't stop, merely walked faster as he made his way through the prison hall.

"Whoa, um, Carretta," Rodrick stammered through one of the doors with a barred window.

"I said take off your clothes and get on your knees, prisoner!" Carretta commanded.

"Y-yea..." Rodrick's answer was lost as Sorin took the stairs two at a time.

Lilith watched the firm line of her husband's ass, enjoying the play of muscles. Sorin had a firm hold on her and she let go of him only to playfully scratch at his flesh.

"Oh, Lord Sorin!" Nan and a couple other servants jumped out of the nobleman's way as he strode past.

Lilith lifted her head and gave the gawking Nan a superior grin, calling, "You act as though you've never seen a naked god before."

He flung around the corners to the climb to the

Black Tower. His fingers dug into her upper thigh, holding her steady. Cream already infused her pussy, making wet and ready for his touch. It had been too long since he made love to her. Her heart ached as she thought of everything she could have lost.

By the time he kicked open the door to his chambers and lowered her to her feet, Lilith's arousal hit full force. She tore at her clothing, pulling the patient issue off her skin. Before the last piece of clothing fell, Sorin lunged forward, tackling her onto the bed. His body pinned hers. Flesh molded to perfect, hot flesh.

"A god?" He grinned at her, his face cast in shadows as there was no fire in the fireplace. "That must make you my goddess." He slid up, then down, forcing her nipples to rub against him. "How should I best worship you, my lady goddess?"

"Love me."

Lilith arched against him as he obeyed. Sorin sucked a breast into his mouth, moaning so loud, vibrations moved over her chest. His tongue swirled the nipple, forcing it to peak between his lips. A hand slipped between her thighs to tantalize the aroused clit he found there.

She undulated her hips against him, trying to tempt his finger to press inside her slick pussy. How could he have so much control? Her body felt like it was on fire. She gripped his arms, digging her nails into his flesh, unsure if she tried to pull his body up or push his mouth down.

"I need you inside me," she begged. "Please, Sorin, take me, finish me."

Sorin groaned, trying to keep his head as he moved to the other perfect breast. His finger glided between the velvety folds of her sex and he traced the length of it, refusing to dip inside. Lilith gripped him tighter, gasping and panting as she writhed beneath him.

*Not yet...*

Sorin wanted to make sure she never forgot this moment. He bit at her breast, unable to get enough of the soft mound. She opened her legs wider and he pinched the small bud of her sex.

"Ah, please, I'll do anything you want, just finish me." Desperately she bucked against his hand, searching for release.

How could he resist her?

*Fool.*

*Idiot.*

*Weak.*

Sorin grinned, the words not bothering him as they once had. So what if he was a fool for her? Or an idiot to give in to her every demand? What did he care if she, his beautiful goddess, his wife, was his one weakness? She loved him. Nothing else mattered.

Sorin buried himself in the sweet glide of her pussy, giving her what they both wanted. She squeezed his cock with her sex, the muscles surrounding him like a tight sheath. He rocked his hips in a shallow thrust.

"More," she groaned, clawing at his ass. "Hard."

Sorin let loose an animalistic growl as he pulled back only to slam forward. She moaned in loud pleasure. He did it again and again, pausing with each forceful thrust.

"More," she commanded, her hands roaming his body in haphazard, nail-scratching patterns. "Fast. Take me. Finish me."

He lifted up, bracing his weight on his arms. His knee slid up to settle beneath her thigh. Sorin pounded his hips, giving her what she begged for. She inched along the bed but he merely followed her with his hips, driving in and out at a frantic pace. Whatever the doctors had given him worked. He felt strong and alive. With each joining of their hips, he grunted. Her sweet warmth took every inch, so soft and wet against his hard size. Sweat beaded his flesh and his stomach muscles began to burn from the frantic excursion, but he couldn't stop.

Lilith cried out, tensing in beautiful release. Her pussy quivered and gripped his shaft. The sensations were too much. His yell muffled hers as he came, spending his seed deep inside her. He jerked uncontrollably as she milked every last bit of it.

Weak, he fell onto the bed next to her, careful not to crush her with his weight. Lilith rolled onto her side, breathing hard. After a long moment passed and his heart began to slow, she said, "I demand that you finish me like that every night."

He chuckled in contentment. Tapping the end of her nose with his finger, he said, "Yea, my lady, an order I will gladly follow. I shall also finish you in the morn." He drew his finger over her parted lips, tracing her delicate features. "Twice in the afternoon. Before the evening meal. Whenever I see you across the courtyard. Whenever I think of you and must seek you out."

"Maybe we should never leave the bed," she giggled, the sound the sweetest music he'd ever heard.

"Mm." He cupped a breast, lazily weighing it in

his palm. "Perhaps that would be best. I will just have to figure out how to do my duty while I'm trapped in your bed, doing my, ah, *duty*."

She gripped his hair, forcing him to look at her. His hand paused on her chest at her serious expression. "I want a life with you, a long, long life. I know you must fight, but no more rushing off into battle on your own. You have earned your honor, my lord, and you have earned the right to be happy. I want to give you that happiness and I want you around to share in mine. I want a family and a home."

"Family?" His knee nudged her thigh and his brow lifted in question.

"No, I'm not." She blushed and he found it endearing. "Divinity issued me a BCP ring to prevent pregnancy, but I had the doctors dissolve it. They said the ring's effect should be reversed fully in a month's time."

"Then I'd better hurry." He massaged the globe beneath his hand. "We do not have much time."

"Hurry?" Her round eyes looked up at him, confused. "Do you want me to have the ring put back? If you don't want children—"

"Of course I wish for children, I merely wish to practice more." He grabbed her hip and slid her next to him. "And it will take me time to have a castle built. My lady wishes for her own home and I intend to give her one. I will have Firewall rebuilt and it can be any way you wish it to be."

"But, the portal is here and I'm supposed to—"

"Sh." He silenced her with his lips. "You think too much, wife. I can see your mind working behind those bewitching eyes of yours. But now is not the time for thinking, now is the time for feeling."

Lilith opened her mouth to speak, but he didn't give her a chance. Sorin crawled down her body and pushed her legs apart. Her sex still glistened from her release and he grinned in anticipation.

# EPILOGUE

"By all the bloody, mace-wielding wenches! I told you they were going to set me afire!" Lilith cursed, hitting at her skirts. Her favorite gown was ruined, burnt by the torch a drunk Lady Alana had dropped during her spin around the center bonfire. Sorin pulled her away from the giant flames. They grew taller as the townsfolk threw wood onto the inferno, rising above the prairie outside the gates of Battlewar Town. "I knew a fire ceremony would include fire, but—"

"My lady," Sorin laughed. "It's a small singe."

"This plane is dangerous, my lord." Lilith gave up on her skirts and poked at his chest, only to walk her finger across a naked pectoral to slide lightly along his arm next to a fresh tattoo. "I see you have regained your manhood."

"And a scar!" He turned, showing her a cut along his back. The superficial wound was only one of the very few marring his smooth flesh.

"You fell off the balancing beam, didn't you?" She laughed.

"It is still fairly won." Sorin pretended to frown at her teasing.

"And a beautiful one at that." She smiled, kissing his back, away from the small cut.

"I have news of Karre, Paige and Jayne," he said, yelling louder as music rose over the earth.

"Tell me later for I know in my heart they are well." Grabbing his hand, she bounced as a musical beat rained over them. Lilith had never been so happy. She had the excitement of talking about other planes with Divinity employees and a life with Sorin that made her complete. "Twirl with me around the fire, my love."

Sorin complied. The motion wasn't really dancing, but more of a lively spin in the firelight that wouldn't stop until they couldn't breathe and their hearts beat wildly in their chests. Lifting her off the ground, Sorin held her to his chest, carrying her as he twirled. "It would seem the gods were not set on punishing me after all."

## The End

# FIGHTING LADY JAYNE

## THE SERIES CONTINUES

Divinity Warriors Book Two
by Michelle M. Pillow

*Alternate Reality Romance*

Jayne Hart has earned her independence by becoming Divinity Corporation's inter-dimensional boxing champion. Life is great, until a dirty fighter knocks her unconscious. Now, abandoned by the corporation in a parallel world, Jayne will use every weapon she has to be free once more. Even if it means running from her sexy new "husband" and spending the rest of her life in a primitive forest.

Ronen of Firewall longs for a woman to warm his bed and his home, but he had no intention of choosing a bride. In an unprecedented move, one chooses him. Never in the history of the marriage ceremony has a woman dared to lay claim. How can he resist the alluring Lady Jayne? She's confident and sure in her decision to be with him—until their wedding night when she's nowhere to be found. But, Ronen is not one to shy from a battle. He will find Jayne and, when he does, he has one particular "weapon" in mind for taming his seductive, wayward wife.

## Extended Prologue Excerpt

Getting her teeth knocked around in her head hurt like hell, but being able to spit blood into the face of her opponent more than made up for the discomfort. Jayne "The Sweet" Hart laughed as Big Bobby Bishop sputtered in anger. She knew he expected her to cry at the landed blow. Truth be, part of Jayne did want to cry. She wasn't a glutton for a beating, and that last hit had left blood running out of her mouth at a steady flow. They'd been going at it for nearly a half hour, bare-knuckle boxing—no protective gear beyond any sanctioned bioengineering, no referees, not like some of the other dimensions had. No, here on dimensional plane 241 almost anything was legal. That's why the gladiator ring paid such big money and drew the notice of rich, inter-dimensional travelers who could afford a private plane jump through Divinity Corporation. It's also why Jayne agreed to travel from her own world to this alternate reality where laws were more of a suggestion and killing someone in a fight was considered a good thing.

In many ways, each alternate reality was like drifting through time on her own home plane, had a singular event on the timeline been changed. Each dimension seemed to be a different outcome to a similar historical start. Some were so technologically advanced everything was done for them, and they'd found a worldwide peace and understanding. Jayne generally stayed away from those levels of existence. There wasn't much employment for fighters in such realities.

Other planes hadn't even developed a means of fast communication beyond throwing a bird into the air with a tiny letter tied to its leg. Still others had just installed their first aqueducts or invented their first vehicles to run without horses or oxen. Or, like 241, they had every technological comfort and yet somehow managed to maintain their barbarian sensibilities.

Any way you looked at it, Earth was Earth, just different versions of itself—same languages, matching natural events, some people looked the same but weren't. Humans, for the most part, still resembled humans. And those with power were still greedy bastards trying to tell her how to do her job.

Big Bobby watched her expectantly, his mouth opened as if to scream in victory at any second. Jayne knew he expected her to fall with that punch. She watched as the excitement slowly died from his eyes, replaced by shock, then confusion, until finally a boiling rage. His eyes scanned the crowd before moving toward the large balcony to where his daddy sat watching. Big Bobby's father and known gangster boss had undoubtedly assured his halfwit-of-a-lugnut son that he was a sure winner. It wouldn't have been so bad if Big Bobby had been an admirable opponent, but after a half hour, she could still see out of one of her eyes, and he only managed to knock her off her feet twice.

And Bossman Bishop wanted her to take a dive to this chump?

Jayne snorted. Not bloody likely. She'd never work as a boxer again—not that she had to. In her home dimension, she had plenty of money to bide her twelve lifetimes.

Divinity Corp paid her big for this fight. They were her ticket home and had the only known source of inter-dimensional travel technology on this plane. Natural slips were extremely rare and the timing of them completely predictable by the company, even if they didn't know where the slip would go. If they didn't take her home, she'd be stuck until the end of time. Besides, there was no way she was taking a dive just because the local gangsters had promised to...

What had Bossman said again? Oh, yeah. They were going to gang rape her grandma while she watched. It had hardly been a threat. Jayne was an orphan. Still, a part of her was up in arms for the hypothetical grandmother they'd threatened.

There was no way Bossman could know about her lack of family. The publicity put out by Divinity Corp's entertainment division fostered the whole-some image of their Sweetheart Jayne. Of course, it was all a lie. They hired a family to take pictures with her at a rented country home—the devoted mother, the fake twin sister with a poor health condition, the baby brother and suit 'n' cravat dad.

The loud, almost fanatical cheering of the crowd grew. They surrounded on all sides, lining the rows upon rows of rotating theater seats. Every few minutes, the seats would shift, changing the angle from which a person watched. Lights flashed all around her. Floating cameras zipped by her head, but she ignored them. Most of the bets were on her and she never lost a fight. Never. And she would be damned if she gave this guy the reputation of being the one person who could take her down. He didn't deserve the title or her respect. Rage grew within her that he even dared to presume he was worthy of taking her down.

*Do it for your family, Jayne,* she thought sardonically.

Jayne decided to teach him and Bossman a lesson. She drew her body around, preparing to kick him upside the head in a move she knew he wouldn't see coming. Big Bobby swung again. She dodged the blow, and this time his hand merely grazed her cheek, stinging the cut she had there. She didn't hesitate. Whipping her leg around, she swung it for his head. Suddenly, every nerve in her body exploded with pain. There was no stopping her body's momentum as it lifted off the hard mat. The noise of the crowd faded and grew until stopping altogether. Big Bobby caught her suddenly slowed foot and pushed her backward. Nothing was as it should be. Lights streaked in her vision before her body was abruptly stopped by a metal pole slamming into her back. Then, darkness clouded her mind and she could only think one thing.

*Boxers' Poison.*

For a complete, up-to-date booklist, visit www. MichellePillow.com

# ABOUT MICHELLE M. PILLOW

***New York Times* & *USA TODAY*
Bestselling Author**

Michelle loves to travel and try new things, whether it's a paranormal investigation of an old Vaudeville Theatre or climbing Mayan temples in Belize. She believes life is an adventure fueled by copious amounts of coffee.

Newly relocated to the American South, Michelle is involved in various film and documentary projects with her talented director husband. She is mom to a fantastic artist. And she's managed by a dog and cat who make sure she's meeting her deadlines.

For the most part she can be found wearing pajama pants and working in her office. There may or may not be dancing. It's all part of the creative process.

## Come say hello! Michelle loves talking with readers on social media!

www.MichellePillow.com

facebook.com/AuthorMichellePillow

twitter.com/michellepillow

instagram.com/michellempillow

bookbub.com/authors/michelle-m-pillow

goodreads.com/Michelle_Pillow

amazon.com/author/michellepillow

youtube.com/michellepillow

pinterest.com/michellepillow

# COMPLIMENTARY EXCERPTS

## TRY BEFORE YOU BUY!

# KEEPING PAIGE

## BY MICHELLE M. PILLOW

Divinity Warriors Book Three
*Alternate Reality Romance*

An outcast because of her psychic abilities, Paige doesn't expect her people to rescue her when a zealous sect of Faerians sacrifices her to their gods. Thrown through a fairy ring to a new dimensional plane, drugged on ambrosia, she is compelled to claim the first man she meets. Only when the effects wear off and she's left with a husband expecting more than she's willing to give, does Paige discover the true extent of what the fairies have done.

Ordered by the king to marry, Sir Aidan of Fallenrock is dead set against taking a bartered bride. He believes his people should be patient and wait for the gods to bless them. When the beautiful Lady Paige comes through the sacred rings, kissing and touching him like she knows their joined fate, Aidan's sure he's being rewarded—until his new bride tries to back out of their marriage.

## Keeping Paige Prologue Excerpt

*Great Forest, Faerian Territory, Parallel Universe*

"Oh, blessed fairies of the great forest, givers of spring, and givers of life after the cold! Take our autumn offering to grant us safe winter and bring life after the snow. Take our offered sister and make her a queen of your realm."

"Let me go, you crazed heretics!" Paige screamed, kicking and jerking her limbs to be free of the hands that held her high over a sea of ivy-crowned heads. Outrage pumped hard and fast through her veins until she felt as if her heart might burst from her chest in little pieces. "You don't want me. I'm not a believer. I will curse you with dead trees and wilted flowers. My father's people will not stand for this!"

All right, so the last part was a lie. Her father's people wouldn't care what the Faerians did to her. In fact, she half expected they traded her to the crazed women to be rid of the last of her cursed family. How else would the heretics have known where her hunting ground was located? Or that she'd be there following the buck migration.

The Faerians ignored her pleas and threats, answering the priestess's words with random exclamations of, "Oh, blessed fairies!" and "Take our Forestter sister. Grant us life!"

Long, drifting branches passed over her, the yellowed leaves falling with each push of the breeze. They hit her chest and hips, and fluttered onto the female heads surrounding her only to tangle in their flowing locks. A tiny giggle mingled amongst the swaying treetops and Paige stiffened in horror. Soon the first laugh was followed by more mischievous sounds, as if a choir of fairies watched the procession. She couldn't see them, but that didn't mean they weren't there and very real.

Paige didn't need to see the ground or the pathway in which they traveled to know what was happening. They took her to the sacred circle, to the fairy ring of the great forest to be sacrificed. The trees gave way to a grassy clearing. A ring of stone pillars created a large circle, each roughly carved and three times as tall as the women. Their towering height imposed as it impressed. The believers carried Paige between two of the pillars.

"At least give me back the clothes you stole from me. Don't send me like this!" she screamed, shaking now that they were drawing to the end of the journey. Everyone knew about the fairy rings, had been warned as children to avoid stepping within the fairy playground. Paige's own grandmother claimed to have come through them when she was a young girl. "At least give me my bow. Have some compassion. Don't send me to the fairy world unarmed."

Paige believed in the possibility of fairies, though she had never seen one for herself. From what she had been told as a child, they were mischievous, somewhat vengeful creatures and they liked nothing more than to play tricks on non-worshippers.

"Oh, blessed fairies, here is our sister!" the priestess called. The woman ordered her lowered and Paige felt the cold chill of a stone altar at her naked back. The flimsy gauze they'd wrapped around her waist like a belt hardly counted as clothing. As the material snagged on the rock, the pin holding it close to her hips dug into her flesh.

Paige struggled to be free. A ring of mushrooms grew in the center of the stones, so innocuous in appearance that if a person didn't know about their hidden magic they might be tempted to step inside. Was this truly the fairy ring, supposed doorway to fairy realm? The truth was Paige didn't know where the ring would lead. No one did. She doubted even the Faerian priestess knew all the fairy secrets. Her grandmother came through and it wasn't the fairy world she had been living in.

The priestess stood over her as countless hands pinned Paige down. The woman's white gown formed tight to her bodice only to flow in long waves along her waist and hips. The skirt trailed behind her in a long train. Tiny gold flowers were embroidered along the hem. Her followers wore the same outfit, minus the embroidery and train. Long, straight black hair seemed to stir around the priestess's oval face, the thin strands dancing like snakes. The woman lifted a wooden cup she had carried with her from the village.

"Drink of the ambrosia," the priestess urged, her gorgeous brown eyes round and filled with promise. "Taste the nectar of the fairy goddess and feel the pleasures of old magic. Let it take you. Let it show you."

Paige clenched her mouth tight, struggling violently as fingers pressed into her cheeks to force her teeth apart. The priestess's expression didn't change as she leaned over and slowly poured the cup's contents into her prisoner's mouth. Wherever the liquid touched, tingling erupted, almost burning in its intensity.

Paige tried to resist, spitting the liquid out over her face, but it was too much. She was forced to choke down several gulps or drown. The tingling spread down her throat into her stomach and over her cheeks from where trails of discarded liquid touched her flesh. She tried to resist the alluring magic, but it was as useless as resisting the falling rain.

The instant the cup was empty the Faerian women let go, leaving her free to run. Paige shot up on the altar, ready to bolt into the woods to hide, only to be brought short by a transparent winged creature flying in front of her face. Paige jerked back in fright, sliding her ass on the rough stone. The fairy's gown matched that of the priestess, with the train trailing down past her feet as she fluttered about in the air. The creature's eyes looked too big for her face and her skin glimmered, tinged with pale blues and silvers. Silver threads wove in delicate patterns over her wings. Soon more small beings began to appear to her, each tinted with different shades of nature.

Paige couldn't move. The strange sensation of the

ambrosia traveled through her blood, leaving her stomach to conquer her limbs. Even her fingernails and hair seemed to prickle. With each passing second, the fairies became clearer. They flew around the gathered worshipers, perching on their shoulders and heads, completely unseen by those who did not drink. Several pulled at the priestess's hair, combing the locks with their fingers to create the snakelike effect she had noticed earlier.

They buzzed around her and Paige jerked, trying to follow them with her eyes. But, when she looked too quickly, the forest blurred into streaks of impossible colors. The Faerians became excited at Paige's apparent visions.

"What madness is this," Paige whispered, swatting at the pests. The flat of her hand managed to smack one across the body and send it flying. Instantly, the others became enraged and attacked. Though Paige tried to fight them off, they swarmed her, pinching her flesh, pulling the long locks of her red hair and the gauze of her belt, pushing wherever they could touch—along the soles of her feet, her exposed sex, her nose and breasts. Paige grunted, flailing about in an effort to be free. With surprising strength, the fairies slid her ass over the coarse surface of stone toward the center ring. For a moment they held her suspended in the air before tossing her at the ground into the ring of mushrooms.

Paige screamed for salvation, but the only answer she received was the high-pitched screech of fairy laughter and the incessant droning of, "Oh, blessed fairies! Take our sister, grant us life!"

For a complete, up-to-date booklist, visit www. MichellePillow.com

# TAKING KARRE

## BY MICHELLE M. PILLOW

Divinity Warriors Book Four
*Alternate Reality Romance*

Sir Vidar of Spearhead is too busy guarding the borderlands to bother with the headache of selecting a bride. Ordered to marry by the king, he plans to grab a woman and get back to the warfront, never to think of it again. That is until he meets the alluring Lady Karre with her teasing eyes, lush lips and irresistible ways.

Known by many names, inter-dimensional thief Karre, has only one purpose—take down the company that ruined her life. When her luck runs out and she's caught, Divinity Corporation condemns her to matrimony on a primitive, warrior-filled plane where Karre soon discovers there are worse fates than being prisoner to a man with insatiable appetites.

Before long, days and nights filled with bliss becomes something neither expected, and when Karre is taken, Vidar is forced to confront emotions a battle-hardened warrior never expected to feel.

## Taking Karre Prologue Excerpt

*Three weeks ago, Dimensional Plane 395, Adult Pleasure Centre VWH*
*Because right now, in this moment, she was their fantasy.*

Karre marched out on stage in red stiletto heels, a slinky dress, big grin and nothing else. She kept tempo with the hard, drumming beat of music. Men hollered, whooping their excitement just to see her. She smiled at them, looking over the crowd of heads. She could make them do anything—beg, buy, steal, kill—because right now, in this moment, she was their fantasy.

Blonde hair piled high on her head, garnished with a string of diamonds and rubies some suitor had given her. It was a sweet trinket, one she might even keep, not that she would remember where the jewels came from. She traveled too much and had more important things on her mind.

Karre turned slowly with her arms raised above her head. The hem of her short dress lifted to just below the curve of her ass. When her back was to the crowd, she bent forward. The cheering grew as the men got a peek of the naked treasure hidden beneath the clinging silver. What did she care if they saw her ass? Her pussy? Her breasts? They were just skin, flesh, a tool like any other. No matter how much they wanted her, they would never be able to touch her.

On this dimensional plane of existence, humans cohabitated with humanoid creatures. The first time Karre saw a vampire sucking on the neck of a shifted werewolf, she'd nearly sprinted out of the room to find her wrist portal to flash out of there to another plane. The portable device looked like a large bracelet to most, but to Karre it was her sole means of survival.

Necessity made her stay where she was. This plane was the easiest to get jewels on without resorting to thievery and the hard, shiny rocks were good for trade in nearly every dimension. Besides, not counting the dancing, being in Dimensional Plane 395 was like taking a vacation. With so many strange and different creatures, they never questioned anything she said and most were focused more on blood-drinking and pleasure-seeking.

Being in a new dimensional plane was like being in your world, but only if had it evolved in a different way. To a point, there were many similarities. Languages, generally, were relatively similar, though for some reason the written word consisted of unfamiliar symbols. Some people looked the same, but were not the same people. Natural disasters and major human events were shared. Weather was the same and each place was still Earth.

"I adore you, Sparkle!" a man yelled. "Marry me!"

Karre turned to look over her shoulder at the crowd and winked. A plethora of large green horns, red flesh, reptile skin, webbed fingers, sharp fangs, and ridged flesh stretched out before her until the mass became a single entity flowing back and forth like a wave.

"I'll take that as a yes," the same voice answered her playful flirting. A rush of similar proposals followed the first, showering her in declarations of love. But she wasn't fool enough to believe them. What they felt wasn't love. It was lust.

Karre knew their adoration for what it was and

used it to fuel her dance. She twirled and wiggled, thrust her ass toward them, drew her hips in seductive circles, only to pause in a sexy pose in time with the music. Slowly, she undressed, peeling the slinky gown off her body. Several lights flashed, illuminating her from various angles, leaving no curve unseen.

Just flesh. Just a means. Just another job. Just another plane and soon a distant memory.

Her smile widened, as she knew this was her last dance, at least for this trip. The cheering rose, but she stopped listening. And then it was over. Karre held still, letting the dying notes find their silence before walking naked from the stage.

"You were wonderful tonight, Sparkle," a new dancer fawned. "The crowd loves you. I was wondering if you'd show me how to—"

"Is he here?" Karre asked, stopping the woman from starting a conversation Karre didn't have time for. It's not like she could tell the truth—that all her dancing skill was someone else's memories uploaded into her brain by a device she'd bartered for on another plane.

"He's in your room," the woman answered, frowning slightly at having her question dismissed.

"And he brought a large case. I think it's full of gifts so you'll consider his suit."

"Perfect," Karre grinned. Taking a long robe the woman held out, she slipped it over her shoulders. "I don't want to be disturbed."

*Two weeks ago, Dimensional Plane 154, Stac Lesh Mansion*
*Because right now, in this moment, she was the help.*

Karre stared at her red, curly hair in the liquid-silver reflection wall. It had been pulled into a bun at the nape of her neck. The long skirt of the plain uniform and padded body suit did much to hide her figure under the thick gray wool. An apron, changed every time so much as a spot marred the pristine white, covered high over her chest and low to her knees. With the clothes and makeup to pale her face into an unimpressive mask, no one would look twice in her direction because right now, in this moment, she was the help.

She had expected to keep her head down and do her job for months before coming back into this room. But in putting on the uniform, she became invisible. The rich people she worked for didn't look in her direction twice. Well, that wasn't necessarily true. When the wife was gone, the husband had looked at her more than twice. A big grin showcasing blacked-out teeth and a very inappropriately timed belch had changed his interest quickly.

Karre reached to touch her reflection. Behind her, the rich baby's room spread out like the entrance to a palace. Gilded ceilings etched with clouds, golden rays of light and ridiculously cheerful fat angels stretched above as white marble stretched below. It was cold and unwelcoming and more than any one person deserved.

"Oh, wonderful, finally, help," the rich wife said, sweeping into the room. Karre didn't bother to learn the lady's name. "Rich wife" was much easier to remember. The woman held her child under the arms, away from her chest, as if contact with the baby would somehow ruin her carefully planned outfit. "Which one are you?"

"Brigitte, ma'am."

"Take Cinny," the woman ordered. "Mommy needs time to collect herself."

Karre suppressed her groan of frustration at being interrupted and stood to dutifully take the child. She cradled the poor creature close and walked it toward the crib.

"Sing to Cinny before you put her down," rich wife ordered, standing before the liquid silver as she brushed at her clothes.

Karre stopped walking. Sing? To the gurgling, wiggling mass in her arms?

"Well, Brigitte?"

"Mistress, mistress, let me come in," Karre sang the only childlike-sounding song she could think of at the moment, pausing to clear her throat. "I have the pence if you have a quim."

"What a pretty tune," the woman said. "I've never heard it. What does it mean?"

"My dad sang it to my mom," Karre answered, letting the memories she had uploaded into her mind take over her personality—Brigitte of the Fallen Women, a whore's daughter raised in a brothel, adept at blending into new environments. She left off the word "once" before adding the lie, "I'm not sure what it means."

"Carry on."

"Mistress, mistress, I'm stiff as a pin. I need your..." Karre continued, lowering her voice as the woman left her alone with the gurgling, oblivious child. Stopping, she laid the baby down and said,

"Sorry, kid, it's the only song I knew the words to. But I guess it's all right. I turned out just fine with lots of jewels and pretty things and you're too little to understand what any of it means. You should be more worried about growing up in this place with that mom of yours. Now, if you just be good," she paused and tucked a blanket around the infant's body, "I've got a job to do."

Going back to the wall, Karre again reached for her reflection. She stepped forward, letting the liquid hit her hand. It stung, freezing cold in the warm room. For a moment, she hesitated, glancing back at the gurgling child. She thought about grabbing Cinny and taking the baby with her.

"Sorry, kid," she whispered, "even with that mother, you're better off here."

It was a delicate balance—keeping her purpose in her mind while living out the personality and quirks of another—almost like having two people in her head. Karre's hand met with the wall as she felt around, searching for the device she'd hidden. When her fingers met with a smooth, flat surface, she frowned. Putting a second hand to the wall she became frantic, sliding her palms in wide, searching arcs. Perhaps the adhesive she used had come loose. She bent her knees, crouching as she searched the bottom corner of the liquid reflecting wall. Her fingers were so cold it became hard to feel, but the molecular structure of the liquid kept the silver from trickling down her arms as it remained bonded to itself.

Then, to her great surprise, warmth gripped her. A hand wrapped her wrist and jerked her forward. She was pulled through the wall, feeling the sting of silver before landing on a hard, stone floor. Gasping and shivering, she looked around the secret room. A wall of computing towers lined one side, next to three technicians silently typing away on their holographic keypads.

"Lose something, Brigitte?" a man asked, coming close.

Karre glanced up from the floor, "No, sir. I have nothing to lose."

"You are extraordinary." The man laughed. Her eyes instantly took in the familiar insignia of the Divinity Corporation. "Finally, we meet."

Karre forced a grin she didn't feel, letting him see her blackened teeth. Knowing what she looked like, she couldn't help but wonder at his choice of words. Extraordinary? "I wasn't aware we were destined to meet, sir. How lucky for me."

"I can assure you when I'm done with you, you

won't feel lucky." The man leaned down, studying her face. He had the militant rigidity of a soldier, from the purposeful jerks of his body to the engraved frown lines around his mouth and eyes. His hard gaze bored into her, filling her with cold dread. She, or rather Brigitte, had seen that look in men's eyes before. They were usually the kind to beat a prostitute the second they couldn't get their pricks hard.

"I've heard that one before," she mumbled, pretending to be unimpressed.

"I'm Director Tomes and..." He paused, lifting the small, wrist-wrapping device she'd been searching the liquid-silver wall for. Divinity had the only known source of top-secret inter-dimensional travel technology and they wouldn't like the fact that someone had stolen it. "I have a feeling you know where I am from. It was very naughty of you to borrow our only portable jump prototype. Our scientists will be very interested in seeing how you got it to work. This device will make traveling to uncharted worlds much easier. No more carting around temporary portals. No more perfectly timed pickups from headquarters. No more rescue parties."

*Less supervision so you can do more dark deeds,* Karre silently added.

"We'll be able to explore planes at a much faster rate," Tomes continued, as if it was a good thing.

Just like an infectious disease.

"Sorry, I'm not available for science lessons, but if you'd like to make an appointment, I'm sure I can fit you in," Karre hummed in pretend thought, "uh, never."

"Oh, you're going to be fun to break, my dear," Tomes promised. "Talbert. Get her ready to go."

For a complete, up-to-date booklist, visit www.MichellePillow.com

# PLEASE LEAVE A REVIEW

## THANK YOU FOR READING!

Please take a moment to share your thoughts by reviewing this book.

Be sure to check out Michelle's other titles at www.michellepillow.com